The Sea Witch

The Sea Witch

STEPHEN COONTS

A Tom Doherty Associates Book
New York

THE SEA WITCH

A Forge Book
Published by Tom Doherty Associates, LLC
175 Fifth Avenue
New York, NY 10010

www.tor-forge.com

Forge® is a registered trademark of Tom Doherty Associates, LLC.

Library of Congress Cataloging-in-Publication Data

Coonts, Stephen, 1946–
    The sea witch / Stephen Coonts. — 1st ed.
      p. cm.
    "A Tom Doherty Associates book."
    ISBN 978-0-7653-3231-8 (hardcover)
    ISBN 978-1-4299-6093-9 (e-book)
    1. Undercover operations—Fiction. I. Title.
PS3553.O5796S43 2012
813'.54—dc23

                        2012001816

First Edition: May 2012

Printed in the United States of America

0 9 8 7 6 5 4 3 2 1

To Rachael, Lara, David, and Tyler

CONTENTS

PREFACE

Airplanes have fascinated me since my first airplane ride at the age of six.

The Sea Witch resulted from daydreaming about the PBY Catalina, the most numerous allied seaplane of World War II and the one that made the largest contribution to the allied war effort. Manufactured by Consolidated Aircraft, the Catalina first flew in 1935 and was obsolete by 1941. Still, it was relatively cheap and in production when the war arrived; over four thousand of them were built before production ceased in 1945.

The Catalina had two engines mounted in nacelles on the wing, a fully cantilevered design that was mounted on a pedestal to get the props well above swells and sea spray. The design was continuously updated with more powerful engines, acrylic glass blisters for the waist guns, improved armor and electrical systems, and self-sealing fuel tanks. The first versions were true flying boats, but later in the war retractable wheels were added to some versions so they could land and take off ashore or on water, increasing the plane's utility at the expense of its weight-carrying capacity and range.

Amphibious Catalinas flew into the 1980s as water-bombers and island transports. Even today a few are still flying as toys for the wealthy. Margarita-man Jimmy Buffett owned one for years, as did oceanographer Jacques Cousteau.

Although painfully slow, cruising at about 100 to 110 knots, loud, unheated, unpressurized, and uncomfortable, the flying-boat versions of the Catalina could carry fuel for over twenty hours of flight, giving them extraordinary range. They were used in every imaginable role, including ocean reconnaissance, air-sea rescue, mine-laying, and antisubmarine warfare. A few squadrons in the western Pacific painted their Catalinas flat black and attacked Japanese warships and freighters at night. Between August 1943 and January 1944, Black Cat squadrons sank 112,700 tons of Japanese shipping, damaged another 47,000 tons, and damaged ten warships.

You will find Catalinas at several aviation museums, including the San Diego Air and Space Museum, the Lone Star Flight Museum in Galveston, Texas, and the National Museum of the U.S. Air Force in Dayton, Ohio. The best display, however, is probably at the National Naval Aviation Museum in Pensacola, Florida. A complete restored Cat hangs from the ceiling. Displayed on the floor under it is a cutaway version of the hull, complete with manikin pilots and crewmen, machine guns, a bomb sight, a drift-indicating instrument, radios, bunks, and a coffeepot. You can put your nose right up to the glass and really look.

That display will fire your imagination. You are somewhere over the great ocean on a deep Pacific night, you and your mates have found an enemy ship, and you are going to attack!

The Bell Boeing V-22 Osprey, perhaps the most revolutionary aircraft to enter military service since the first helicopter, is the airplane featured in the novella *Al-Jihad*. A transport that can land and take off vertically, the plane was number one on the U.S. Marines' wish list for a generation, which was how long it took to design, manufacture, test, tinker, and get it into service. The engineering and aerodynamic problems were immense, and, many thought, insolvable. One of the largest was the necessity of keeping the machine aloft if one engine failed: The solution was an automatic transmission that allowed one engine to turn both rotors. The first flight of the Osprey took place in 1989, yet it didn't become operational until 2007, eighteen years later. The machine takes full advantage of the latest computer technology to help it remain aloft and controllable.

With two turboprop engines mounted on the ends of the wings, the Osprey has a unique look. One must be both a fixed-wing and helicopter pilot to fly it. I had the good fortune to fly the simulator in the late 1990s, an experience that eventually led to *Al-Jihad*. I also used the V-22 in the novel *Cuba*, published in 1999.

The 17th Day was a short story that came from my fascination with World War I aviation. I have always wanted to write a novel about WWI aviators, but it hasn't happened yet.

The planes of the Great War were little more than flying shipping crates. Made of wood, fabric, piano wire, and engines that weren't ready for prime time, they flew without armor, self-sealing fuel tanks, or, except late in the war, oxygen for the pilots. The fabric was treated with a chemical called dope to tighten it up, and the stuff burned easily. In fact, the whole plane was a flying matchhead, especially when the fuel tank was spewing gasoline from bullet holes onto the hot parts of the engine. Amazingly, the pilots and gunner/observers flew without parachutes.

The planes were also difficult to fly. These machines did not fly like the Cessnas and Pipers of our day. The margin between their stall speed and maximum airspeed was often painfully thin, which led to a great many stall/spin accidents, inevitably fatal. None of these WWI machines had brakes, merely a steerable tail skid. They had no altitude instruments, no electrical system, and only a rudimentary compass.

Aeronautical engineering was still an occult art when these planes were designed, mostly by eye. If it looked about right, they gave it to a test pilot to see if he could get it off the ground. Even the designs that made it into service had a depressing habit of shedding wings in dives or turns and having fabric peel off.

Early scouts flew with rotary engines, which had good power-to-weight ratios. The spinning engine—yes, the whole engine revolved around a fixed crankshaft—acted like a giant flywheel, imparting a tremendous torque to the airframe, which had to be overcome by design features and pilot input on the controls. These airplanes turned well in one direction, with the torque assisting, and poorly in the other.

The rotary engine had many technical limitations, however, not the least of which was a very real limit to how big such an engine could be when mounted and flown on the airframes of the day. More complex water-cooled in-line engines replaced the rotaries. Needless to say, the science of designing reliable internal combustion engines was also in its infancy, so these motors had a deplorable tendency to quit in flight.

The Royal Aircraft Factory S.E.5A (for Scout Experimental Model 5A), which is featured in *The 17th Day*, was powered by a French-built 200-HP Hispano-Suiza V-8 engine, one manufactured under wartime conditions with poor metallurgy. Still, the airframe was soundly designed, stable, and the machine made a good gun platform. Although it wasn't as maneuverable as other designs, the S.E.5A was fast, capable of about 138 mph in level flight. It carried one synchronized belt-fed .303-caliber machine gun that fired through the prop arc and a Lewis gun with a fifty-round ammo tray on a Foster mount placed above the wing so it could fire over the prop arc.

Today the best place to see World War I aircraft—originals and modern copies—in flight is the Old Rhinebeck Aerodrome in Rhinebeck, New York. The facility also has the best static collection I have ever seen of these airplanes and the biplanes of the 1920s. For that we have the late Cole Palen to thank.

Airplanes, adventures, life and death in the skies . . .

Come on, strap in and we'll go flying.

Stephen Coonts

The Sea Witch

ONE

"I'm looking," the skipper said, flipping through my logbook, "but I can't find any seaplane time." The skipper was Commander Martin Jones. His face was greasy from perspiration and he looked exhausted.

"I've had four or five rides in a PBY," I told him, "but always as a passenger." In fact, a PBY had just brought me here from Guadalcanal. It departed after delivering me, some mail, and a couple of tons of spare parts.

The Old Man gave me The Look.

"You're a dive-bomber pilot. What in hell are you doing in a Black Cat squadron?"

"It's a long story." Boy, was that ever the truth!

"I haven't got time for a long story," Jones said as he tossed the logbook on the wardroom table and reached for my service record. "Gimme the punch line." Aboard this small seaplane tender, the wardroom doubled as the ship's office.

"They said I was crazy."

That comment hung in the air like a wet fart. I leaned against the edge of the table to steady myself.

Hanging on her anchor, the tender was rolling a bit in the swell coming up the river from Namoia Bay, on the southwestern tip of New Guinea where the Owen Stanley Mountains ran into the sea. The only human habitation within two hundred miles was a village, Samarai, across the bay on an island. The sailors on the tender never went over there, nor was there any reason they should. If Namoia Bay wasn't the end of the earth, believe me, you could see it from here.

The commander flipped through my service record, scanning the entries. "Are you crazy?"

"No more than most," I replied. Proclaiming your sanity was a bit like proclaiming your virtue—highly suspect.

"This tender can support three PBYs," Commander Jones said, not looking at me. "We launch them late in the afternoon, and they hunt Jap ships at night, return sometime after dawn. Three days ago one of our birds didn't come back." He looked up, straight into my eyes. "The crew is somewhere out there," he swept his hand from left to right, "dead or alive. We'll look for them, of course, but the South Pacific is a big place, and there is a war on."

"Yes, sir."

"Until we get another plane from Australia, we'll only have two birds to carry the load."

I nodded.

"One of our copilots is sick with malaria, too bad to fly. You will fly in his place unless you've really flipped out or something."

"I'm fine, sir."

"Why did they get rid of you?"

"The Japs shot three SBDs out from under me, killed two of my gunners. The skipper said he couldn't afford me. So here I am."

The Old Man lit a cigarette and blew the smoke out through his nose.

"Tell me about it."

So I told it. We launched off the carrier one morning on a routine search mission and found a Jap destroyer in the slot, running north at flank speed. When the lookouts spotted us the destroyer captain cranked the helm full over, threw that can into as tight a circle as it would turn while every gun let loose at us. There were four of us in SBDs; I was flying as number three. As I rolled into my dive I put out the dive brakes, as usual, and dropped the landing gear.

With the dive brakes out the Dauntless goes down in an eighty-degree dive at about 250 knots. Takes a couple thousand feet to pull out. With the dive brakes and gear out, prop in flat pitch, she goes down at 150, vibrating like a banjo string. Still, you have all day to dope the wind and sweeten your aim, and you can pickle the bomb at a thousand feet, put the damn thing right down the smokestack before you have to pull out. Of course, while you are coming down like the angel of doom the Japs are blazing away with everything they have, and when you pull out of the dive you have no speed, so you are something of a sitting duck. You also run the risk of overcooling the engine, which is liable to stall when you pour the coal to it. Still, when you really want a hit . . .

I got that destroyer—the other three guys in my flight missed. I put my thousand-pounder right between the smokestacks and blew that can clean in half. It was a hell of a fine sight. Only the Japs had holed my engine, and it quit on the pullout, stopped dead. Oil was blowing all over the windshield, and I couldn't see anything dead ahead. Didn't matter—all that was out there was ocean.

My gunner and I rode the plane into the water. He hit his head or something and didn't get out of the plane, which sank before I could get him unstrapped.

I floated in the water, watched the front half of the destroyer quickly sink and the ass end burn. None of the Japs came after me. I rode my little life raft for a couple days before a PBY landed in the open sea and dragged me in through a waist-gun blister. With all the swells I didn't think he could get airborne again, but he did, somehow.

A couple days later the ship sent a half dozen planes to Henderson Field to operate from there. I figured Henderson could not be tougher to land on than a carrier and was reasonably dry land, so I volunteered. About a week later I tangled with some Zeros at fifteen thousand feet during a raid. I got one and others got me. Killed my new gunner, too. I bailed out and landed in the water right off the beach.

Jones was reading a note in my record while I talked. "Your commanding officer said you shot down a Zero on your first pass," Jones commented, "then disobeyed standing orders and turned to reengage. Four Zeros shot your Dauntless to pieces."

"Yes, sir."

"He says you like combat, like it a lot."

I didn't say anything to that.

"He said you love it."

"That's bullshit."

"Bullshit, sir."

"Sir."

"He says he pulled you out of SBDs to save your sorry ass."

"I read it, sir."

"So tell me the rest of it."

I took a deep breath, then began. "Six days ago another Zero shot me down after I dive-bombed a little freighter near Bougainville. I got the Maru all right, but as I pulled out and sucked up the gear a Zero swarmed all over me and shot the hell out of the plane, punched a bunch of holes in the gas tanks. There wasn't much I could do about it at 150 knots. My gunner got him, finally, but about fifty miles from Henderson Field we used the last of our gas. I put it in the water and we floated for a day and a half before a PT boat found us."

"Leaking fuel like that, were you worried about catching fire?" Commander Jones asked, watching me to see how I answered that.

"Yes, sir. We were match-head close."

He dropped his eyes. "Go on," he said.

"Kenny Ross, the skipper, was pissed. Said if I couldn't dive-bomb like everyone else and get hits, he didn't want me.

"I told him everyone else was missing—I was getting the hits, and I'd do whatever it took to keep getting them, which I guess wasn't exactly the answer he wanted to hear. He canned me."

The Black Cat squadron commander stubbed out his cigarette and lit another.

He rubbed his eyes, sucked a bit on the weed, then said, "I don't have anyone else, so you're our new copilot. You'll fly with Lieutenant Modahl. He's probably working on his plane. He wanted to go out this morning and look for our missing crew, but I wouldn't let him go without a copilot." The skipper glanced at his watch. "Go find him and send him in to see me."

"Aye, aye, sir."

"Around here everybody does it my way," he added pointedly, staring into my face. "If I don't like the cut of your jib, bucko, you'll be the permanent night anchor-watch officer aboard this tender until the war is over or you die of old age, whichever happens first. Got that?"

"Yes, sir."

"Welcome aboard."

. . .

The tender was about the size of a Panamanian banana boat, which it might have been at one time. It certainly wasn't new, and it wasn't a Navy design. It had a big crane amidships for hoisting planes from the water. That day they were using the crane to lower bombs onto a float.

A plane was moored alongside, covered with a swarm of men. They had portable work stands in place around each engine and tarps rigged underneath to keep tools and parts from falling in the water.

Five-hundred-pound bombs were being loaded on racks under the big Catalina's wings. Standing there watching, I was amazed at the size of the bird—darn near as big as the tender, it seemed. The wingspan, I knew, was 104 feet, longer than a B-17.

The plane was painted black; not a glossy, shiny, raven's-feather black, but a dull, flat, light-absorbing black. I had never seen anything uglier. On the nose was a white outline of a witch riding a broomstick, and under the art, the name *Sea Witch*.

The air reeked, a mixture of the aromas of the rotting vegetation and dead fish that were floating amid the roots of the mangrove trees growing almost on the water's edge. The freshwater coming down the river kept the mangroves going, apparently, although the fish had been unable to withstand the avgas, oil, and grease that were regularly spilled in the water.

At least there was a bit of a breeze to keep the bugs at bay. The place must be a hellhole when the wind didn't blow!

None of the sailors working on the Cat wore a shirt, and many had cut off the legs of their dungarees. They were brown as nuts.

One of the men standing on the float winching the bombs up was wearing a swimsuit and tennis shoes—nothing else. I figured he was the officer, and after a minute or so of watching I was sure. He was helping with the job, but he was also directing the others.

"Lieutenant Modahl?"

He turned to look at me.

"I'm your new copilot."

After he got the second bomb on that wing, he clambered up the rope net that was hung over the side of the ship. When he was on deck he shook my hand. I told him my name, where I was from.

He asked a few questions about my experience, and I told him I'd never flown seaplanes—been flying the SBD Dauntless.

Modahl was taller than me by a bunch, over six feet. He must have weighed at least two hundred, and none of it looked like fat. He about broke my hand shaking it. I thought maybe he had played college football. He had black eyes and black hair, filthy hands with ground-in grease and broken fingernails. Only after he shook my hand did it occur to him to wipe the grease off his hands, which he did with a rag that had been lying nearby on the deck. He didn't smile, not once.

I figured if he could fly and fight, it didn't matter whether he smiled or not. Anyone in the South Pacific who was making friends just then didn't understand the situation.

MODAHL:

The ensign was the sorriest specimen I had laid eyes on in a long time. About five feet four inches tall, he had poorly cut, flaming red hair, freckles, jug ears, and buckteeth. He looked maybe sixteen. His khakis didn't fit, were sweat-stained and rumpled—hell, they were just plain dirty.

He mumbled his words, didn't have much to say, kept glancing at the Cat, didn't look me in the eyes.

Joe Snyder and his crew were missing, Harvey Deets was lying in his bunk shivering himself to death with malaria, and I wound up with this kid as a copilot, one who had never even *flown* a seaplane! Why didn't they just put one of the storekeepers in the right seat? Hell, why didn't we just leave the damn seat empty?

No wonder the goddamn Japs were kicking our butts all over the Pacific.

The kid mumbled something about Jones wanting to see me. If the Old Man thought I was going to wet-nurse this kid, he was going to find out different before he got very much older.

I told the kid where to put his gear, then headed for the wardroom to find Commander Jones.

After Modahl went below, I climbed down the net to look over the Black Cat. The high wing sported two engines. The wing was raised well over the fuselage by a pedestal, which had been the key innovation of the design. The mechanic or flight engineer, I knew, had his station in the pedestal. The Cat had side blisters with a fifty-caliber on a swivel-mount in each, a thirty-caliber which fired aft through a tunnel, and a flexible thirty in a nose turret.

This Cat, however, had something I had never seen before. Four blast tubes covered with condoms protruded from the nose under the bow turret. I entered the Cat through one of the open blisters and went forward for a look. The bunk compartment was where passengers always rode; I had never been forward of that.

I went through a small watertight hatch—open now, of course—into the compartment used by the radio operator and the navigator. The radio gear took up all the space on the starboard side of the compartment, while the navigator had a table with a large compass mounted on the aft end. He had boxes for stowage of charts and a light mounted right over the table. The rear bulkhead was covered with a power distribution panel.

Three steps led up to the mechanic's seat on the wing support pylon. The mech had a bunch of levers and switches up there to control the engines and cowl flaps in flight.

On forward was the cockpit, with raised seats for the pilot and copilot. The yokes were joined together on a cross-cockpit boom, so when one moved, the other did also. On the yoke was a set of light switches that told the mechanic what the pilot wanted him to do. They were labeled with things like, "Raise floats" and "Lower floats," which meant the wingtip floats, and directions for controlling the fuel mixture to the engines. The throttle and prop controls were mounted on the overhead.

The cockpit had windows on both sides and in the roof, all of which were open, but still, it was stifling in there with the heat and stink of rotting fish. The Catalina was also rocking a bit in the swell, which didn't help either.

The door to the bow compartment was between the pilot and copilot, below the instrument panel. One of the sailors was there installing ammo in the bow gun feed trays. He explained the setup.

Four fifty-caliber machine guns were mounted as tightly as possible in the bow compartment—the bombsight had been removed to make room and the bombardier's window plated over with sheet metal. Most of the space the guns didn't occupy was taken up by ammo feed trays. The trigger for the guns was on the pilot's yoke. The remainder of the space, and there wasn't much, was for the bow gunner, who had to straddle the fifties to fire the flexible thirty-caliber in the bow turret. Burlap bags were laid over the fixed fifties to protect the gunner from burns.

The sailor showing me the installation was pretty proud of it. His name was Hoffman. He was the bow gunner and bombardier, he said, and had just finished loading ammo in the trays. Through the gaps in the trays I could see the gleam of brass. Hoffman straddled the guns and opened the hatch in the top of the turret to let in some air and light.

"That hatch is open when you make an attack?" I asked.

"Yes, sir. Little drafty, but the visibility is great."

The Cat bobbing against the float and the heat in that closed space made me about half-seasick. I figured I was good for about one more minute.

"How do they work?" I asked, patting the guns.

"They're the Cat's nuts, sir. They really pour out the lead. They'll cut a hole in a ship's side in seconds. I hose the thirty around to keep their heads down while Mr. Modahl guts 'em."

"He goes after the Japs, does he?"

"Yes, sir. He says we gotta do it or somebody else will have to. Now me, I'd rather be sitting in the drugstore at Pismo Beach drinking sodas with my girl while someone else does the heavy lifting, but it isn't working out that way."

"I guess not."

"In fact, when we dive for those Jap ships, and I'm sitting on those guns, I'd rather be somewhere else, anywhere at all. I haven't peed my pants yet, but it's been close."

"Uh-huh."

"Guess everybody feels that way."

"Hard to get used to."

"Are you going to be flying with us?"

"I'm flying copilot for a while. They told me Deets has malaria."

"You know Cats, huh?"

"I don't know a damn thing about flying boats. I figure I can learn, though."

Hoffman wasn't thrilled, I could see that. If I were him, I would have wanted experienced people in the cockpit, too.

Oh well, how tough could it be? It wasn't like we were going to have to land this thing on a carrier deck.

HOFFMAN:

This ensign wasn't just wet behind the ears— he was dripping all over the deck. Our new copilot? He looked like he just got out of the eighth grade. What in hell were the Zeros thinking?

That wasn't me you heard laughin', not by a damn sight. It wasn't very funny. This ensign must be what's on the bottom of the barrel.

It was like we had already lost the war; we were risking our butts with an idiot pilot who thought he could win the war all by himself, and if it went bad, we had a copilot who's never flown a seaplane—hell, a copilot who oughta be in junior high—to get our sorry asses home.

I patted those fifties, then crawled aft, out of the bow compartment, before I embarrassed myself by losing my breakfast. There seemed to be a tiny breeze through the cockpit, and that helped. That and the sunlight and the feeling I wasn't closed up in a tight place.

There were lots of discolored places on the left side of the fuselage. I asked Hoffman about that. He looked vaguely surprised. "Patches, sir. Japs shot up the *Witch* pretty bad. Killed the radioman and left waist gunner. Mr. Modahl got us home, but it was a close thing."

Hoffman went aft to get out of the airplane, leaving me in the cockpit. I climbed into the right seat and looked things over, fingered all the switches and levers, studied everything. The more I could learn now, the easier the first flight would be.

Everything looked straightforward . . . no surprises, really. But it was a big, complicated plane. The lighting and intercom panels were on the bulkhead behind the pilots' seats. There were no landing gear or flap handles, of course. Constant speed props, throttles, RPM and manifold pressure gauges . . . I thought I could handle it. All I needed would be a little coaching on the takeoff and landing.

The button on the pilot's yoke that fired the fifties was an add-on, merely clamped to the yoke. A wire from the button disappeared into the bow compartment.

I gingerly moved the controls, just a tad, while I kept my right hand on the throttles. Yeah, I could handle it. She would be slow and ponderous, nothing like a Dauntless, but hell, flying is flying.

I climbed out and stood on the float watching the guys finish loading and fusing the bombs. Three men were also sitting on the wing completing the fueling. I climbed up the net to the tender's deck and leaned on the rail, looking her over.

Modahl came walking down the deck, saw me, and came over. He had sort of a funny look on his face. "Okay," he said, and didn't say anything else.

He leaned on the rail, too, stood surveying the airplane.

"Nice plane," I remarked, trying to be funny.

"Yeah. Commander Jones says we can leave as soon as we're ready. When the guys are finished fueling and arming the plane, I think I'll have them fed, then we'll go."

"Yes, sir. Where to?"

"Jones and I thought we might as well run up to Buka and Rabaul and see what's in the harbor. Moon's almost full tonight—be a shame to waste it. Intelligence thinks there are about a dozen Jap ships at Rabaul, which is fairly well defended. We ought to send at least two Cats. Would if we had them, but we don't."

"Buka?"

"No one knows. The harbor might contain a fleet, or it might be empty."

"Okay."

"Tomorrow morning we'll see if we can find Joe Snyder."

"Where was Snyder going the night he disappeared?"

"Buka and Rabaul," Modahl replied, and climbed down the net to check the fuses on the weapons.

TWO

While the other guys were doing all the work, I went to my stateroom and threw my stuff in the top bunk. Another officer was there, stripped to his skivvies in the jungle heat. He was seated at the only desk writing a long letter—he already had four or five pages of dense handwriting lying in front of him.

"I'm the new guy," I told him, "going to be Modahl's copilot."

He looked me over like I was a steer he was going to bid upon. "I'm Modahl's navigator, Rufus Pottinger."

"We're flying together, I guess."

I couldn't think of a thing to say. I wondered if that letter was to a girl or his mother. I guessed his mother—Pottinger didn't strike me as the romantic type, but you can never tell. There is someone for everyone, they say.

That thought got me thinking about my family. I didn't have a solitary soul to write to. I guess I was jealous of Pottinger. I stripped to my skivvies and asked him where the head was.

He looked at his watch. "You're in luck. The water will be on in fifteen minutes. For fifteen minutes. The skipper of this scow is miserly with the water."

I took a cake of soap, a towel, and a toothbrush and went to to visit the facilities.

POTTINGER:

I'd heard of this guy. They had thrown him out of SBDs, sent him to PBYs. I guess that was an indicator of where we stood on the naval aviation totem pole.

The scuttlebutt was this ensign was some kind of suicidal maniac. You'd never know it to look at him. With flaming red hair, splotchy skin, and buckteeth, he was the kind of guy nobody ever paid much attention to.

He also had an annoying habit of failing to meet your gaze when he spoke to you—I noticed that right off. Not a guy with a great future in the Navy. The man had no presence.

I threw my pen on the desk and stretched. I got to thinking about Modahl and couldn't go on with my letter, so I folded it and put in in the drawer.

Modahl was a warrior to his fingertips. He also

took crazy chances. Sure, you gotta go for it—that's combat. Still, you must use good sense. Stay alive to fight again tomorrow. I tried to tell him that dead men don't win wars, and he just laughed.

Now the ensign had been added to the mix. I confess, I was worried. At least Harvey Deets had curbed some of Modahl's wilder instincts. This ensign was a screwball with no brains, according to the rumor, which came straight from the yeoman in the captain's office who saw the message traffic.

In truth I wasn't cut out for this life. I was certainly no warrior—not like Modahl, or even this crazy redheaded ensign. Didn't have the nerves for it.

I wasn't sleeping much those days, couldn't eat, couldn't stop my hands from shaking. It sounds crazy, but I knew there was a bullet out there waiting for me. I knew I wasn't going to survive the war. The Japs were going to kill me.

And I didn't know if they would do it tonight, or tomorrow night, or some night after. But they would do it. I felt like a man on death row, waiting for the warden to come for me.

I couldn't say that in my letters home, of course. Mom would worry herself silly. But Jesus, I didn't know if I could screw up the courage to keep on going.

I hoped I wouldn't crack, wouldn't lose my manhood in front of Modahl and the others.

I guess I'd rather be dead than humiliate my-self that way.

Modahl knew how I felt. I think he sensed it when I tried to talk some sense into him.

Oh, God, be with us tonight.

I sat through the brief and kept my ensign's mouth firmly shut. The others asked questions, especially Modahl, while I sort of half listened and thought about that great big ocean out there.

The distances involved were enormous. Buka on the northern tip of Bougainville was about 400 nautical miles away, Rabaul on the eastern tip of New Britain, about 450. This was the first time I would be flying the ocean without my plotting board, which felt strange. No way around it though—Catalinas carried a navigator, who was supposed to get you there and back. Modahl apparently thought Pottinger could handle it—and I guess he had so far.

Standing on the tender's deck, I surveyed the sky. The usual noon shower had dissipated, and now there was only the late-afternoon cumulus building over the ocean.

Behind me I could hear the crew whispering—of course they weren't thrilled at having a copilot without experience, but I wasn't either. I would have given any-thing right then to be manning a Dauntless on the deck of *Enterprise* rather than climbing into this heaving, stinking, ugly flying boat moored in the mouth of this jungle river.

The *Sea Witch*! Gimme a break!

The evening was hot, humid, with only an occasional puff of wind. The tender had so little freshwater it came out of the tap in a trickle, hardly enough to wet a washrag. I had taken a sponge bath, which was a wasted effort. I was already sodden. At least in the plane we would be free of the bugs that swarmed over us in the muggy air.

I was wearing khakis; Modahl was togged out in a pair of Aussie shorts and a khaki shirt with the sleeves rolled up—the only reason he wore that shirt instead of a tee shirt was to have a pocket for pens and cigarettes. Both of us wore pistols on web belts around our waists.

As I went down the net I overheard the word "crazy." That steamed me, but there wasn't anything I could do about it.

If they wanted to think I was nuts, let 'em. As long as they did their jobs it really didn't matter what they thought. Even if it did piss me off.

I got strapped into the right seat without help, but I was of little use to Modahl. I shouldn't have worried. The copilot was merely there to flip switches the pilot couldn't reach, provide extra muscle on the unboosted controls, and talk to the pilot to keep him awake in the middle of the night. I didn't figure Modahl would leave the plane to me and the autopilot on this first flight. To-night, the bunks where members of the crew normally took turns napping were covered with a dozen flares and a dozen hundred-pound bombs, to be dumped out the tunnel hole aft.

The mechanic helped start the engines, Pratt & Whitney 1830s of twelve hundred horsepower each. That sounded like a lot, but the Cat was a huge plane, carrying four five-hundred-pound bombs on the racks, the hundred-pounders on the bunks, several hundred pounds of flares, God knows how much machine gun ammo, and fifteen hundred gallons of gasoline, which weighed nine thousand pounds. The plane could have carried more gas, but this load was plenty, enough to keep us airborne for over twenty hours.

I had no idea what the Cat weighed with all this stuff, and I suspect Modahl didn't either. I said something to the mechanic, Dutch Amme, as we stood on the float waiting our turn to board, and he said the weight didn't matter. "As long as the thing'll float, it'll fly."

With Amme ready to start the engines, Modahl yelled to Hoffman to release the bowlines. Hoffman was standing on the chine on the left side of the bow. He flipped the line off the cleat, crawled across the nose to the other chine, got rid of that line, then climbed into the nose turret through the open hatch.

A dozen or so of the tender sailors pushed us away from the float. As soon as the bow began to swing, Amme began cranking the engine closest to the tender. It caught and blew a cloud of white smoke, and kept the nose swinging. Modahl pushed the rudder full over and pulled the yoke back into his lap as Amme cranked the second engine.

In less time than it takes to tell, we were taxiing away from the tender.

"You guys did that well," I remarked.

"Practice," Modahl said.

Everyone checked in on the intercom, and there was a lot of chatter as they checked systems, all while we were taxiing toward the river's mouth.

Finally, Modahl used the rudder and starboard engine to initiate a turn to kill time while the engines came up to temperature. The mechanic talked about the engines—temps and so on; Modahl listened and said little.

After two complete turns, the pilot closed the window on his side and told me to do the same. He flipped the signal light to tell Amme to set the mixtures to Auto Rich. While I was trying to get my window to latch, he straightened the rudder and matched the throttles. Props full forward, he pulled the yoke back into his lap and began adding power.

The engines began to sing.

The *Witch* accelerated slowly as Modahl steadily advanced the throttles while the flight engineer called out the manifold pressures and RPMs. He had the throttles full forward when the nose of the big Cat rose, and she began planing the smooth water in the lee of the point. Modahl centered the yoke with both hands to keep us on the step.

I glanced at the airspeed from time to time. We were so heavy I began to wonder if we could ever get off. We passed fifty miles per hour still planing, worked slowly to fifty-five, then sixty, the engines howling at full power.

It took almost a minute to get to sixty-five with that heavy load, but when we did Modahl pulled the yoke back into his lap and the Cat broke free of the water. He eased the yoke forward, held her just a few feet over the water in ground effect as our airspeed increased. When we had eighty on the dial Modahl inched the yoke back slightly, and the *Witch* swam upward in the warm air.

"When the water is a little rougher or there is a breeze, she'll come off easier," he told me. He flipped the switch to tell Amme to raise the wingtip floats.

He climbed all the way to a thousand feet before he lowered the nose and pulled the throttles back to cruise manifold pressure, then the props back to cruise RPM. Of course, he had to readjust the throttles and sync the props. Finally he got the props perfectly in snyc, and the engine noise became a smooth, loud hum.

After Modahl trimmed he hand-flew the *Witch* awhile. We went out past the point, where he turned and set a course for the tip of the island that lay to the northeast.

"Landing this thing is a piece of cake. It's a power-on landing into smooth water: Just set up the attitude and a bit of a sink rate and ease her down and on. In the open sea we full-stall her in. After you watch me do a few I'll let you try it. Maybe tomorrow evening if we aren't going out again."

"Yeah," I said. The fact that Modahl was making plans for tomorrow was comforting somehow, as I'm sure it was to the rest of the crew, who were listening on the intercom. As if we were a road repair gang on the way to fill a pothole.

When we got to the island northeast of Samarai, we flew along the water's edge for twenty minutes, looking

for people or a crashed airplane or a signal—anything—
hoping our lost Catalina crew had made it this far.

We had been in the air over an hour when Modahl
turned northeast for Bougainville. He engaged the autopilot and sat for a while watching it fly the plane. We were
indicating 115 miles per hour, about a hundred knots.
The wind was out of the west. Pottinger, the navigator,
was watching the surface of the sea to establish our drift
before sunset.

"Keep your eyes peeled, gang, for Joe Snyder and his
guys. Sing out if you see anything."

The land was out of sight behind and the sun was
sinking into the sea haze when Modahl finally put his
feet up on the instrument panel and lit a cigarette. The
sun on our left stern quarter illuminated the clouds,
which covered about half the sky. The cloud bases were
at least a thousand feet above us, the tops several thousand feet above that. The visibility was about twenty
miles, I thought, as I studied the sun-dappled surface of
the sea with binoculars.

Standing in the space behind us, between the seats,
the radioman also studied the sea's surface. His name
was something Varitek . . . I hadn't caught his first name.
Everyone called him Varitek, even the other sailors.

The noise level in the plane was high; the headsets
made it tolerable. Barely. Still, the drone of the engines
and the clouds flamed by the setting sun and the changing patterns on the sea were very pleasant. We had cracked
our side windows so there was a decent breeze flowing
into the plane.

One of the sailors brought us coffee, hot and black. As Modahl smoked cigarettes, one after another, we sat there watching the colors of the clouds change and the sea grow dark. A sliver of the sun was still above the horizon when I got my first glimpse of the moon, round and golden, climbing the sky.

The other members of the crew were disappointed that they didn't see any trace of Snyder's plane. I hadn't thought they would, nor, apparently, did Modahl. He said little, merely smoked in silence as the clouds above us lost their evening glow.

"Watch the moonpath," Modahl told me after a while. "Anything we see up this way is Japanese, and fair game." He adjusted the cockpit lighting for night flying and asked the radioman for more coffee.

MODAHL:

I couldn't get Joe Snyder and his crew out of my mind. A fellow shouldn't go forth to slay dragons preoccupied with other things, but I liked Joe, liked him a lot. And whatever happened to him could happen to me and mine.

The Japs were staging ships and supplies through Buka and Rabaul as they tried to kick us off Guadalcanal. They were working up to taking Port Moresby, then invading Australia, when our invasion of Guadal threw a monkey wrench in their plans. Now they were trying to reinforce their forces on Guadalcanal. A steady stream of troop transports and cargo ships had been in and out of those harbors, not to mention destroyers and cruisers, enough to put the fear in everybody. Then there are Jap planes—they had a nice airfield on Rabaul and a little strip near Buka. The legs on the Zeros were so long you just never knew where or when you would encounter them, though they stayed on the ground at night.

If they could have flown at night, the Cats couldn't. The guns in the side blisters were poor defense against enemy fighters. When attacked, the best defense was to get as close to the sea as possible so the Zeros couldn't make shooting passes without the danger of flying into the water. If a Japanese pilot ever slowed down and lined up behind a Cat a few feet over the water, he'd be meat on the table for the blister gunners—the Japs had yet to make that mistake and probably never would.

I sat there listening to the engines, wondering what happened to Joe, if he were still alive, if he would ever be found.

VARITEK:

If you didn't believe you had a good chance of living through the flight, you would never get aboard the plane. Somebody said that to me once, and it was absolutely true. It took guts to sit through the brief and man up and ride through a takeoff, knowing how big this ocean was, knowing that your life was dependent on the continued function of this cunning contraption of steel and duraluminum. Knowing your continued existence depended on the skill of your pilot.

On Modahl.

Modahl. If he made one bad decision, we were all dead.

These other guys, I saw them fingering rosaries or moving their lips in prayer. I didn't buy any of that sweet-hereafter Living on a Cloud Playing a Harp bullshit.

This is it, baby. This life is all you get. When it's over, it's over. And you ain't coming back as a cow or a dog or a flea on an elephant's ass.

I tried not to think about it, but the truth was, I was scared. Yeah, I believed in Modahl. He was a good officer and a good pilot. Sort of a holier-than-thou human being, not a regular kind of guy you'd like to drink beer with, but I didn't care about that. None of these officers were going to be your buddy, and who would want them to? Modahl could fly that winged boat. He was good at that, and that was all that mattered. That and the fact that he could get us home.

He could do that. Modahl could. He could get this plane and his ass and the asses of all of us home again, back to the tender.

Yeah.

HOFFMAN:

These other guys were so calm that afternoon, but I wasn't. Tell you the truth, I was scared. Waiting, waiting, waiting . . . it was enough to make a guy puke. I tried to eat and managed to get something down, but I upchucked it before we manned up.

I knew the guys on the Snyder crew—went to boot camp with a couple of them and shipped out with them to the South Pacific. Yeah, they were good guys, *guys just like me,* and they were dead now. Or floating around in the ocean waiting to die. Or marooned on an island somewhere. The folks at home saw the pictures in *Life* and thought tropical paradise, but these islands were hellholes of jungle, bugs, and snakes, with green shit growing right down to the water's edge. Everything was alive, and everything would eat you.

And the South Pacific was crawling with Japs. The sons of Nippon didn't take prisoners, the guys said, just tortured you for information, then whacked off your head with one of those old swords. Gave me the shivers just thinking about it.

If they captured me . . . well, *Jesus!*

No wonder I was puking like a soldier on a two-week drunk.

I just prayed that Modahl would get us home. One more time.

POTTINGER:

This evening the wind was only a few knots out of the west-southwest. Our ground speed was, I estimated, 102 knots. We were precisely here on the chart, at this spot I marked with a tiny x. If I had doped the wind right. Beside the x I noted the time.

Later, as we approach Bougainville, Modahl would climb above the clouds and let me shoot the stars for an accurate fix. Of course, once we found the island, I would use it to plot running fixes.

I liked the precision of navigation. The answers were real, clear, and unequivocal, and could be determined with finest mathematical exactness. On the other hand, flying was more like playing a musical instrument. I could determine Modahl's mood by the way he handled the plane. Most of the time he treated it with the utmost respect, working the plane in the wind and sea like a mae-stro directing a symphony. When he was preoc-cupied, like tonight, Modahl just pounded the keys, horsed it around, never got in sync with it.

He was thinking about Joe Snyder's crew, I fig-ured, wondering, pondering life and death.

Death was out there tonight, on that wide sea or in those enemy harbors.

It was always there, always a possibility when we set out on one of those long flights into the unknown.

The torture was not combat, a few intense min-utes of bullets and bombs; torture was the waiting. The hours of waiting. The days. The nights. Wait-ing, wondering . . .

Sometimes the bullets and bombs came as almost a relief after all that waiting.

The *Sea Witch* was Modahl's weapon. The rest of us were tiny cogs in his machine, living parts. We would live or die as the fates willed it, and whichever way it came out didn't matter as long as Modahl struck the blow.

But the men had faith he'll take them home. Afterward.

I *wanted* to believe that. The others also. But I knew it wasn't true. Death was out there—I could feel it.

Modahl was only a man.

A man who wondered about Joe Snyder and probably had little faith in himself.

Was Modahl crazy, or was it us, who believed?

Nothing in this life was as black as a night at sea. You can tell people that, and they would nod, but no one could know how mercilessly dark a night could be until he saw the night sea for himself.

After the twilight was completely gone that night there was only the occasional flicker of the moonpath through gaps in the clouds, and now and then a glimpse of the stars. And the red lights on the instrument panel. Nothing else. The universe was as dark as the grave.

Modahl eased his butt in his seat, readjusted his feet on the instrument panel, tried to find a comfortable position, and reached for his cigarettes. The pack was empty; he crumpled it in disgust.

"You married?" he asked me.

"No."

"I am," he said, and rooted around in his flight bag for another pack of Luckies. He got one out, fired it off, then rearranged himself, settling back in.

He checked the compass, tapped the altimeter, glanced at his watch, and said nothing.

"Can I walk around a little?" I asked.

"Sure."

I got unstrapped and left him there, smoking, his feet on the panel.

The beat of the engines made the ship a living thing. Everything you touched vibrated; even the air seemed to pulsate. The waist and tunnel gunners were watching out the blisters, scratching, smoking, whatever. Pottinger was working on his chart, the radioman and bombardier were playing with the radar, Amme the mechanic was in his tower making entries in his logbooks.

I took a leak, drank a half a cup of coffee while I watched the two guys working with the radar, and asked some questions. The presentation was merely a line on a cathode-ray tube—a ship, they said, would show up as a spike on the line. Maybe. Range was perhaps twenty miles, when the sea conditions were right.

"Have you ever seen a ship on that thing?" I asked.

"Oh, yeah," the radioman said, then realized I was an officer and added a "sir."

I finished the coffee, then climbed back into the copilot's seat.

When my headset was plugged in again, I asked Modahl, "Do you ever have trouble staying awake?"

He shook his head no.

A half hour later he got out of his seat, took off his headset, and shouted in my ear: "I'm going to get some coffee, walk around. If the autopilot craps out, I'll feel it. Just hold course and heading."

"Yes, sir."

He left, and there I was, all alone in the cockpit of a PBY Catalina over the South Pacific at night, hunting Jap ships.

Right.

I put my feet up on the panel like Modahl had and sat watching the instruments, just in case the autopilot did decide that it had done enough work tonight. The clouds were breaking up as we went north, so every few seconds I stole a glance down the moonpath, just in case. It was about seventy degrees to the right of our nose. I knew the guys were watching it from the starboard blister, but I looked anyway.

We had been airborne for a bit over four hours. We had lost time searching the coast of that island, so I figured we had another hour to fly before we reached Buka. Maybe Modahl was talking to Pottinger about that now.

If my old man could only see me in this cockpit. When he lost the farm about eight years ago, five years after Mom died, he took my sister and me to town and turned us over to the sheriff. Said he couldn't feed us.

He kissed us both, then walked out the door. That was the last time I ever saw him.

Life defeated him. Beat him down.

Maybe someday, when the war was over, I'd try to find him. My sister and I weren't really adopted, just farmed out as foster kids, so legally he was still my dad.

My sister was killed last year in a car wreck, so he was the only one I had left. I didn't even know if he or Mom had brothers or sisters.

I was sitting there thinking about those days when I heard one sharp, hard word in my ears.

"Contact."

That was the radioman on the intercom. "We have a contact, fifteen miles, ten degrees left."

In about ten seconds Modahl charged into the cockpit and threw himself into the left seat.

"I've got it," he said, and twisted the autopilot steering. We turned about fifty degrees left before he leveled the wings.

"We'll go west, look for them on the moonpath, figure out what we've got."

He reached behind him and twisted the volume knob on the intercom panel so everyone could clearly hear his voice. "Wake up, people. We have a contact. We're maneuvering to put it on the moonpath for a visual."

"What do you think it is?"

"May just be stray electrons—that radar isn't anything to bet money on. If it's a ship, though, it's Japanese."

THREE

"We've lost the contact," Varitek, the radioman, told Modahl. "It's too far starboard for the radar."

"Okay. We'll turn toward it after a bit, so let me know when you get it again."

He leaned over and shouted at me. "It's no stray electron. Ghost images tend to stay on the screen regardless of how we turn."

He was fidgety. He got out the binoculars, looked down the moonpath.

He was doing that when he said, "I've got it. Something, anyway." He turned the plane, banking steeply to put the contact ahead of us.

As we were in the turn, he said, "It's a submarine, I think."

As he leveled the wings the radioman shouted, "Contact."

Modahl looked with binoculars. "It's a sub conning tower. About six miles. Running southeast, I think. We're in his stern quarter."

He banked the plane steeply right, then disengaged the autopilot and lifted the nose and added power. "We'll climb," he said. "Make a diving attack down the moonpath."

"Going to drop a bomb?"

"One, I think. There may be nothing at Buka or Rabaul."

He explained what he wanted to the crew over the intercom. "We'll use the guns on the conning tower," he said, "then drop the bomb as we go over. You guys in the blisters and tunnel, hit 'em with all you got as we go by. They'll go under before we can make another run, so let's make this one count."

Everyone put on life vests, just in case.

"Your job," Modahl said to me, "is to watch the altimeter and keep me from flying into the water. I want an altitude callout every ten seconds or so. Not every hundred feet, but every ten seconds."

"Yessir."

He called Hoffman to the cockpit and talked to him. "One bomb, the call will be 'ready, ready, now.' I'll pickle it off, but to make sure it goes, I want you to push your pickle when I do."

"Aye aye, sir."

MODAHL:

The theory was simple enough: We were climbing to about twenty-five hundred feet, if I could get that high under those patchy clouds, then we would fly down the moonpath toward that sub. We'd see him, but he couldn't see us. At two miles I'd chop the throttles and dive. If everything went right, we'd be doing almost 250 mph when we passed three hundred feet in altitude, about a thousand feet from the sub, and I opened fire with the nose fifties.

I planned to pull out right over the conning tower and release the bomb. If I judged it right and the bomb didn't hang up on the rack, maybe it would hit close enough to the sub to damage its hull.

On pullout the guys in the back would sting the sub with their fifties.

Getting it all together would be the trick.

HOFFMAN:

I opened the hatch on the bow turret and climbed astraddle of those fifties. I patted those babies. I'd cleaned and greased and loaded them—if they jammed when we needed them Modahl would be royally pissed. Dutch Amme, the crew chief, would sign me up for a strangulation. Modahl was a nice enough guy, for an officer, but he and Amme wouldn't tolerate a fuck-up at a time like this, which was okay by me. None of us came all this way to wave at the bastards as we flew by.

The guns *would* work—I *knew* they would.

POTTINGER:

We know the Japanese sailors are there—they are blissfully unaware of us up here in the darkness. Right now they have their sub on the surface, recharging batteries and running southeast, probably headed for the area off Guadalcanal . . . to hunt for American ships. When they find one, they will torpedo it from ambush.

We call it war but it's really murder, isn't it? Us or them, whoever pulls the trigger, no matter. The object of the game is to assassinate the other guy before he can do it to you.

We're like Al Capone's enforcers, out to whack the enemy unawares. For the greater glory of our side.

Modahl climbed to the west, with the moon at his back. He got to twenty-four hundred feet before he tickled the bottom of a cloud, so he stayed there and got us back to cruising speed before he started his turn to the left. He turned about 160 degrees, let me fly the *Witch* while he used the binoculars.

"We've got it again," the radioman said. "Thirty degrees left, right at the limits of the gimbals."

"Range?"

"Twelve miles."

"Come left ten," Modahl told me.

I concentrated fiercely on the instruments, holding altitude and turning to the heading he wanted. The Catalina was heavy on the controls, but not outrageously so. I'd call it lots of stability.

The seconds crept by. All the tiredness that I had felt just minutes before was gone. I was ready.

"I've got it," he said flatly, staring through the binoculars. "Turn up the moonpath."

I did so.

"Okay, everybody. Range about eight miles. Three minutes, then we dive to attack."

I tried to look over the nose, which was difficult in a Catalina.

"Still heading southeast," Modahl murmured. "You'll have to turn slightly right to keep it in the moonpath."

The turn also moved the nose so it wouldn't obstruct Modahl's vision.

Maybe I shouldn't have, but I wondered about those guys on that sub. If we pulled this off, these were their last few minutes of life. I guess few of us ever know when the end is near. Which is good, I suppose, since we all have to die.

The final seconds ticked away, then Modahl laid down the binoculars and reached for the controls. He secured the autopilot, and told me, "I'm going to run the trim full nose down. As we come off target, your job is to start cranking the trim back or I'll never be able to hold the nose up as our speed drops."

"Okay."

He retarded the throttles a little, then advanced the props to the stops so they wouldn't act as dive brakes. Still, nose down as we were, we began to accelerate. Modahl ran the trim wheel forward. I called altitudes.

"Two thousand . . . nineteen hundred . . . eighteen . . ."

Glancing up, I saw the conning tower of the sub and the wake it made. I must have expected it to look larger, because the fact that it was so tiny surprised me.

"Twelve . . . eleven . . ."

The airspeed needle crept past 200 mph. We were diving for a spot just short of the sub so Modahl could raise the nose slightly and hammer them, then pull up to avoid crashing.

I could see the tower plainly now in the reflection of the moonlight, which made a long white ribbon of the wake.

"Six hundred . . . five . . . four-twenty-five . . ."

We were up to almost 250 mph, and Modahl was flattening his dive, from about twenty degrees nose down to fifteen or sixteen. He had the tower of that sub boresighted now.

"Three-fifty . . ."

"Three hundred . . ."

"Ready," Modahl said for Varitek's benefit. He shoved the throttles full forward.

"Two-fifty . . ."

Modahl jabbed the red button on the yoke with his right thumb. Even with the shielding the blast tubes provided, the muzzle flashes were so bright that I almost visually lost the sub. The engines at full power were stupendously loud, but the jackhammer pounding just inches from my feet made the cockpit floor tremble like a leaf in a gale.

HOFFMAN:

I could see the sub's tower, see how we were hurtling through the darkness toward that little metal thing amid the swells. When the guns beneath me suddenly began hammering, the noise almost deafened me. I was expecting it, and yet, I wasn't.

I had been pointing the thirty at the Jap, now I held the trigger down.

The noise and heat and gas from the cycling breechblocks made it almost impossible to breathe. This was the fourth time I had done this, and it wasn't getting any better. I could scarcely breathe, the noise was off the scale, my flesh and bones vibrated. The burlap under me insulated me from the worst of the heat, yet if Modahl kept the triggers down, he was going to fry me. I was sitting on hellfire.

And I was screaming with joy . . . Despite everything, the experience was sublime.

"One hundred." I shouted the altitude over the bedlam. Some fool was screaming on the intercom, the engines were roaring at full power, the guns in the nose were hammering in one long, continuous burst . . . I had assumed that Modahl would pull out at a hundred. He didn't.

"Readeee . . ."

"Fifty feet," I shouted over the din, trying to make myself heard. I reached for the yoke.

"Now!" Modahl roared, pushing the bomb release with his left thumb, releasing the gun trigger, and pulling the yoke back into his stomach all at the same time.

I began cranking madly on the trim.

We must have taken the lenses off the periscopes with our keel. I distinctly felt us hit something . . . and the nose was rising through the horizontal, up, up, five degrees, ten, as the guns in the blisters and tunnel got off long rolling bursts. When they fell silent our airspeed was bleeding off rapidly, so Modahl pushed forward on the yoke.

"Hoffman, you asshole, did the bomb go?"

"No, sir. It didn't release."

"You shit. You silly, silly shit."

"Mr. Modahl—"

"Get your miserable ass up here and talk to me, Hoffman."

He cranked the plane around as tightly as he could, but too late. When we got level, inbound, with the moon in front of us, the sub was no longer there. She had dived.

"You fly it," Modahl said disgustedly, and turned the plane over to me.

Hoffman climbed up to stand behind the pilots' seats while Modahl inspected the hung bomb with an Aldis lamp. I tried not to look at the bright light so as to maintain some night vision—the light got me anyway. When Modahl had inspected the offending bomb to his satisfaction and finally killed the light, I was half-blinded.

Hoffman said, "Maybe we got the sub with the guns."

Modahl's lip curled in a vicious sneer, and he turned in his seat, looked at Hoffman as if he were a piece of shit.

"Which side are you on, Hoffman? Your shipmates risked their lives to get that bomb on target, to no avail. If that bomb comes off the rack armed while we're landing, the Japs win and our happy little band of heroes will go to hell together. I don't care if you have to grease those racks with your own blood. When we make an attack they goddamn well better work."

Hoffman still had pimples. When Modahl killed the Aldis lamp I could see them, red and angry, in the glow of the cockpit lights.

"Are you fucking crazy?" Modahl asked without bothering to turn around.

"No, sir," Hoffman stammered.

"Screaming on the intercom during an attack. Jesus! I oughta court-martial your silly ass."

"I'm sorry, sir. It just slipped out. Everything was so loud and—"

Modahl made a gesture, as if he were shooing a fly. But that wasn't the end of it. "Chief Amme," Modahl said on the intercom. "When we get back, I expect you and Hoffman to run the racks through at least a dozen cycles on each bomb station. I want a written report signed by you and Hoffman that the racks work perfectly."

"*Yes, sir.*"

"Pottinger, bring your chart to the cockpit. Let's figure out where we are and where the hell we go from here."

I was still hand-flying the plane, so Modahl said to me, "Head northwest and climb to four thousand, just in case we are closer to Bougainville than I think we are. We'll circle around the northern tip of the island and approach the harbor up the moonpath."

Modahl took off his headset and leaned toward me. "Hoffman's getting his rocks off down there."

"Maybe he's crazy, too," I suggested.

"We all are," Modahl said flatly, and nodded once, sharply. His lips turned down in a frown.

I dropped the subject.

"When you get tired, we'll let Otto fly the *Witch*." Otto was the autopilot. After a few minutes I nodded, and he engaged it.

MODAHL:

Of course Hoffman was crazy. We all were to be out here at night in a flying boat hunting Japs in the world's biggest ocean. Yeah, sure, the Navy sent us here, but every one of us had the wit to have wrangled a nice cushy job somewhere in the States while someone else did the sweating.

It's addictive, like booze and tobacco. I just worried that I'd love it too much. And it's probably a sin. Not that I know much about sin . . . but I can feel the wrongness of it, the evil. That's the attraction, I guess. I liked the adrenaline and the risk and the feeling of . . . power. Liked it too much.

It was two o'clock in the morning when we approached Buka harbor from the sea. Jungle-covered hills surrounded the harbor on two sides. A low spit formed the third side. On the end of the spit stood a small lighthouse. In the moonlight we could see that the harbor was empty. Not a single ship.

Pottinger was standing behind us. "How long up to Rabaul?" Modahl asked.

"An hour and forty-five minutes or so. Depends on how cute you want to be on the approach."

"You know me. I try to be cute enough to stay alive."

"Yeah."

"Before we go, let's wake up the Japs in Buka. Why should they get a good night's sleep if we can't?"

"Think the Japs are still here?"

"You can bet your soul on it."

Modahl pointed out where the town lay, on the in-land side of the harbor. It was completely blacked out, of course.

We made a large, lazy circle while the guys in back readied the parafrags. We would drop them out the tunnel while we flew over the town . . . they fell for a bit, then the parachutes opened, and they drifted unpredictably.

This was a nonprecision attack if there ever was one. It was better than throwing bricks, though not by much.

We flew toward the town at three thousand feet. We were still a mile or so away when antiaircraft tracers began rising out of the darkness around the harbor. The streams of shells went up through our altitude, all right, so they had plenty of gun. They just didn't know where in the darkness we were. The streams waved randomly as the Japs fired burst after burst.

It looked harmless enough, though it wasn't. A shell fired randomly can kill you just as dead as an aimed one if it hits you.

"One minute," Modahl told the guys in back. He directed his next comment at me: "I'm saving the five-hundred-pounders for Rabaul. Surely we'll find a ship there or someplace."

"Thirty seconds."

We were in the tracers now, which bore a slight resemblance to Fourth of July fireworks.

"Drop 'em."

One tracer stream ignited just ahead of us and rose toward us. Modahl turned to avoid it. As I watched the glowing tracers I was well aware of how truly large the Catalina was, a black duraluminum cloud. How could they not hit it?

"That's the last of them." The word from the guys in back came as we passed out of the last of the tracers. The last few bombs would probably land in the jungle. Oh well.

We turned for the open sea. We were well away from

the city when the frags begin exploding. They marched along through the blackness, popping very nicely as every gun in town fell silent.

"Rabaul," Modahl said, and turned the plane over to me.

FOUR

Rabaul!

The place was a legend. Although reputedly not as tough a nut as Truk, the big Jap base in the Carolines, Rabaul was the major Japanese stronghold in the South Pacific. Intelligence said they had several hundred planes—bombers, fighters, float fighters, seaplanes—and from thirty to fifty warships. This concentration of military power was defended with an impressive array of antiaircraft weapons.

The Army Air Corps was bombing Rabaul by day with B-17s, and the Navy was harassing them at night with Catalinas. None of these punches were going to knock them out, but if each blow hurt them a little, drew a little blood, the effect would be cumulative. Or so said the staff experts in Washington and Pearl.

Regardless of whatever else they might be, the Japanese were good soldiers, competent, capable, and ruthless. They probably had bagged Joe Snyder and his crew last night, and tonight, with this moon, they surely knew the Americans were coming.

I wondered if Snyder had attacked Rabaul before he headed for Buka, or vice versa. Whichever, the Japs in Buka probably radioed the news of our 2 A.M. raid to Rabaul. The guys in Rabaul knew how far it was between the two ports, and they had watches. They could probably predict within five minutes when we were going to arrive for the party.

I didn't remark on any of this to Modahl as we flew over the empty moonlit sea; he knew the facts as well as I and could draw his own conclusions. At least the clouds were dissipating. The stars were awe-inspiring.

Pottinger came up to the cockpit with his chart and huddled over it with Modahl. I sat watching the moon-path and monitoring Otto. I figured if Modahl wanted to include me in the strategy session, he would say so. My watch said almost three in the morning. We couldn't get there before four, so we were going to strike within an hour of dawn.

Finally, Modahl held the chart where I could see it, and said, "Here's Rabaul, on the northern coast of New Britain. This peninsula sticking out into the channel forms the western side of the harbor, which is a fine one. There are serious mountains on New Britain and on

New Ireland, the island to the north and east. The highest is over seventy-five hundred feet high, so we want to avoid those.

"Here is what I want to do. We'll motor up the channel between the islands until we get on the moonpath; at this hour of the morning that will make our run in heading a little south of west. Then we'll go in. As luck would have it, that course brings us in over the mouth of the harbor.

"They'll figure we want to do that, but that's the only way I know actually to see what's there. The radar will just show us a bunch of blips that could be anything. If we see a ship we like, we'll climb, then do a diving attack with the engines at idle. Bomb at masthead height. What do you think?"

"Think we'll catch 'em asleep?"

He glanced at me, then dropped his eyes. "No."

"It'll be risky."

"We'll hit the biggest ship in there, whatever that is."

"Five-hundred-pounders won't sink a cruiser."

"The tender was out of thousand-pounders. Snyder took the last one."

"Uh-huh."

"We can cripple 'em, put a cruiser out of the war for a while. Maybe they'll send it back to Japan for repairs. That'll do."

"How about a destroyer? Five hundred pounds of torpex will blow a Jap can in half."

"They got lots of destroyers. Not so many cruisers."

He thought like I did: If there was a cruiser in there,

the Japs knew it was the prime target and they'd be ready; still, that's the one I'd hit. When you're looking for a fight, hit the biggest guy in the bar.

MODAHL:

The kid was right; of course. There was no way we were going to sucker punch the Japs with a hundred-knot PBY. Yet I knew there would be targets in Rabaul so we had to check Buka first.

Snyder not coming back last night was the wild card. If the Japanese had radar at Rabaul, they could take the darkness away from us. Ditto night fighters with radar. Intelligence said they didn't have radar, and we had seen no indications that Intel was wrong, but still, Joe did what we plan to do, and he didn't come home.

Probably flak got him. God knows, in a heavily defended harbor, flying over a couple of dozen warships, the flak was probably thick enough to walk on.

Bombing at masthead height is our only realistic method for delivering the bombs. Hell, we don't even have a bombsight: We took it out when we put in the bow guns. The Catalina is an up-close and personal weapon. We'll stick it in their ear and pull the trigger, which will work, amazingly enough, if we can take advantage of the darkness to surprise them.

We'll pull it off or we won't. That's the truth of it.

POTTINGER:

Talk about going along for the ride: These two go blithely about their bloody work without a thought for the rest of the crew. The have ice water in their veins. And neither asked if damaging a ship was worth the life of every man in this plane. Or anybody's life.

They're assassins, pure and simple, and they thought they were invulnerable.

Of course, the Japanese were assassins, too.

All of these assholes were in it for the blood.

One hundred knots is glacially slow when you're going to a fire. I was so nervous that I had trouble sitting still. Despite my faith in Pottinger's expertise, I kept staring into the darkness, trying to see what was out there. I didn't want to fly into a mountain and these islands certainly had 'em. When Pottinger said we had reached the mouth of the channel between the two, we turned north. Blindly.

As we motored up the channel at two thousand feet, I wondered why I didn't want to put off the moment of truth, till tomorrow night, or next week, or next year. Or forever. I decided that a man needs a future if he is to stay on an even keel, and with Rabaul up ahead, the future was nothing but a coin flip. I wanted it to be over.

Pottinger and Varitek, the radioman, were on the radar; they reported lots of blips. We came up the moonpath and looked with binoculars: We counted twenty-three ships in the harbor, about half of them warships and the rest freighters and tankers. Lots of targets.

"I think the one in the center of the harbor is a cruiser," Modahl said, and passed the binoculars to me. As he turned the plane to the north, to seaward, I turned the focus wheel of the binoculars and studied it through his side window. With the vibration of the plane and the low light level—all we had was moonlight—it was hard to tell. She was big, all right, and long enough, easily the biggest warship in the harbor.

"Looks like a cruiser to me," I agreed. I lost the moon as I tried to focus on other ships. Modahl turned the *Witch* 180 degrees and motored back south. This time the harbor was on my side.

"See anything that looks like a carrier?" he asked.

"I'm looking." Destroyer, destroyer, maybe a small cruiser . . . more destroyers. A sub. No, two subs.

"Two subs, no carrier," I said, still scanning.

"I'd like to bomb a carrier before I die," Modahl muttered. Everyone on the circuit heard that, of course, and I thought he should watch his lip. No use getting the crew in a sweat. But it was his crew, so I let the remark go by.

"The biggest ship I see is the cruiser in the center," I said, and handed back the glasses.

"Surrounded by cans. When they hear us, everyone opens fire, and Vesuvius will erupt under our ass."

"We can always do a destroyer. We can send one or two to the bottom. They are excellent targets."

"I know."

We turned and motored north again. He waited until the moonlight reflected on the harbor and studied it again with the binoculars. Pottinger was standing behind us. He didn't say anything, kept bent over so he could look out at the harbor.

"The cruiser," Modahl said with finality. He told the crew, as if they didn't know, "We are off Rabaul harbor. The Japs have twenty-three ships there, one of which appears to be a cruiser. Radio, send off a contact report. When you're finished we'll attack."

"What do you want me to say, Mr. Modahl?"

"Just what I said. Twenty-three ships, et cetera."

"Yes, sir."

"Tell me when you have an acknowledgment."

The cruiser lay at a forty-five-degree angle to the moonpath, which had to be the direction of our approach since we were bombing visually. To maximize our chances of getting a hit, we should train off the four bombs, that is, drop them one at a time with a set interval between them—we were going to try to drop the bomb that had hung on the rack at Buka. On the other hand, we could do the most damage if we salvoed all four bombs right down the smokestack. The obvious compromise was to salvo them in pairs with an appropriate interval between pairs—that was Modahl's choice. He didn't ask anyone's opinion; he merely announced how we were going to do it.

Hoffman consulted the chart. If we managed to get up to 250 mph at weapons release, an interval of two-tenths of a second would give us seventy-five feet between salvos. Modahl knew the math cold and gave his approval. Hoffman set two-tenths of a second on the interval- ometer.

"How low are you going to go?" Pottinger asked. The cockpit lights reflected in the sweat on his face.

"As low as possible."

"We're going to get caught in the bombs' blast."

"Every foot of altitude increases our chances of miss- ing."

"And of getting home," Pottinger said flatly.

"Get back to your station," Modahl snapped. "The enemy is there, and I intend to hit him."

"I'm merely pointing out the obvious."

"Take it up with Commander Jones the next time you see him."

"*If* I see him."

"Goddamn it, Pottinger! That's *enough*! Get back to your station and shut the fuck up."

The crew heard this exchange, which was one reason Modahl was so infuriated. Right then I would have bet serious money that Modahl and Pottinger would never again fly together.

We flew inbound at three thousand feet. Modahl had climbed higher so he could dive with the engines at idle and still get plenty of airspeed. I was used to the speed of the Dauntless, so motoring inbound toward the proper dive point—waiting, waiting, waiting—was like having poison ivy and being unable to scratch.

"Now," he said, finally, and we both pushed forward

on the yokes as he pulled back the throttles and advanced the prop levers. The engines gurgled . . . and the airspeed began increasing. Modahl ran the trim forward. Down we swooped, accelerating ever so slowly.

The cruiser was dead ahead, anchored, without a single light showing. The black shapes on the silver water, the darkness of the land surrounding the bay, the moon and stars above . . . it was like something from a dream. Or a nightmare.

I called the altitudes. "Nineteen, eighteen, seventeen . . ."

He pushed harder on the yoke, ran the nose trim full down. Speed passing 180, 190 . . .

Every gun in the Jap fleet opened fire, all at once.

"Holy . . . !"

Fortunately, they were all firing straight up or randomly. Nothing aimed our way.

The tracers were so bright I would clearly see everything in the cockpit. The Japs had heard us—they just didn't know where we were. Why they didn't shoot away from the moon was a mystery to me.

"Eleven . . . ten . . . nine . . ."

Even the shore batteries were firing. The whole area was erupting with tracers. And searchlights. Four searchlights came on, began waving back and forth.

A stream of weaving tracers from one of the destroyers flicked our way . . . and I felt the blows as three or four shells hit us trip-hammer fast.

"Five . . . four . . ."

Modahl was flattening out now, pulling on the yoke with all his strength as the evil black shape of the Japanese cruiser rushed toward us. The airspeed indicator needle quivering on 255 . . .

"Three . . ."

"Help me!" he shouted, and lifted his feet to the instrument panel for more leverage.

I grabbed the yoke, braced myself, and pulled. The altimeter passed two hundred . . . I knew there was some lag in the instrument, so we had to be lower . . . The nose was coming up, passing one hundred . . .

We were going to crash into the cruiser! I pulled with all my strength.

"Now!" Modahl shouted, so loud Hoffman could have heard it without earphones.

I felt the bombs come off; two sharp jolts. Dark as it was, I glimpsed the mast of the cruiser as we shot over it, almost close enough to touch.

As that sight registered, the bombs exploded . . . right under us! The blast lifted us, pushed . . .

Modahl rammed the throttles forward to the stops.

The *Witch* wasn't responding properly to the elevators.

"The trim," Modahl said desperately, and I grabbed the wheel and turned it with all my strength. It was still connected, still stiff, so maybe we weren't dead yet.

Just then a searchlight latched on to us, and another. The ghastly glare lit the cockpit.

"Shoot 'em out," Modahl roared to the gunners in the blisters and the tail, who opened fire within a heartbeat.

I was rotating the stiff trim wheel when I felt Modahl push the yoke forward. His hand dropped to mine, stopping the rotation of the trim wheel. Then the fifties in the nose lit off. He had opened fire!

Up ahead . . . a destroyer, shooting in all directions—no, the gunners saw us pinned in the searchlights and swung their guns in our direction!

Modahl held the trigger down—the fifties vibrated like a living thing as we raced toward the destroyer, the engines roaring at full power. With the glare of the searchlight and tracers and all the noise, it looked like we had arrived in hell.

And I could feel shells tearing into us, little thumps that reached me through the seat.

We were rocketing toward the destroyer, which was shooting, shooting, shooting . . .

Another searchlight hit us from the port side, nearly blinding me. Something smashed into the cockpit, the instrument panel seemed to explode. Simultaneously, the bow fifties stopped, and the plane slewed.

Modahl slumped in his seat.

I fought for the yoke, leveled the wings, screamed at that idiot Hoffman to stop firing, because he had opened up with the thirty-caliber as soon as the fifties lit off and was still blazing away, shooting BBs at the elephant: Even though we were pinned like a butterfly in the lights, in some weird way I thought that the muzzle flashes of the little machine gun would give away our position.

My mind wasn't functioning very well. I could hear the fifties in the blisters going, but I shouted, *"Hit the lights, hit the lights"* anyway, praying that the gunners would knock them out before the Japs shot us out of the sky.

We were only a few feet over the black water: The destroyer was right there in front of us, filling the windscreen, strobing streams of lava-hot tracer. I cranked the trim wheel like a madman, trying to get the nose up.

The superstructure of the destroyer blotted out everything else. I turned the trim wheel savagely to raise the nose and felt something impact the plane as we shot over the enemy ship.

More shells tore at us, then the tracer was arcing over our wings. One by one the lights disappeared—I think our gunners got two of them—and, mercifully, we exited the flak.

The port engine was missing, I was standing on the rudder trying to keep the nose straight, and Modahl was bleeding to death.

He coughed black blood up his throat.

Thank God he was off the controls!

Blood ran down his chest. He reached for me, then went limp.

Three hundred feet, slowing . . . at least we were out of the flak.

The gyro was smashed, the compass frozen: The glass was broken. Both airspeed indicators were shot out, only one of the altimeters worked . . .

Everyone was babbling on the intercom. The cruiser was on fire, someone said, bomb blasts and flak had damaged the tail, one of the gunners was down, shot, and—

Modahl was really dead, covered with blood, his eyes staring at his right knee.

The port engine quit.

Fumbling, I feathered the prop on the port engine. If it didn't feather, we were going in the water. Now.

It must have, because the good engine held us in the sky.

We were flying straight at the black peninsula on the western side of the bay. We were only three hundred feet above the ocean. Ahead were hills, trees, rocks, more flak guns—I twisted the yoke and used the rudder to turn the plane to the east.

We'll go down the channel, I thought, then it will be a straight shot south to Namoia Bay. Some islands north of there—if we can't make it home, maybe we can put down near one.

The gunners lifted and pulled Modahl out of the pilot's seat while I fought to get the *Sea Witch* to a thousand feet.

Varitek had caught a piece of flak, which tore a huge gash in his leg and ripped out an artery. The other guys sprinkled it with sulfa powder and tried to stanch the bleeding . . . I could hear the back-and-forth on the intercom, but they didn't seem to think he had much of a chance.

Dutch Amme climbed into the empty pilot's seat. He surveyed the damage with an electric torch, put his fingers in the hole the shell had made that killed Modahl.

There were other holes, five of them, behind the pilot's seat, on the port side. Amazingly, the destroyer hadn't gotten him—someone we had passed had raked us with something about twenty-millimeter size.

"Searchlights . . . That's why Joe Snyder didn't come back."

"Yeah," I said, refusing to break my fierce concentration on the business at hand. I had the Cat out into the channel now, with the dark shape of New Ireland on my left and the hulk of New Britain on the right. From the chart I had seen, that meant we had to be heading south. Only 450 nautical miles to go to safety.

"The hull's tore all to hell," Amme said wearily. "When we land we'll go to the bottom within a minute, I'd say. You'll have to set her down gentle, or we might even break in half on touchdown."

Right! Like I knew how to set her down gently.

Amme talked for a bit about fuel, but I didn't pay much attention. It took all my concentration to hold the plane in a slight bank into the dead engine and keep a steady fifty pounds or so of pressure on the rudder, a task made none the easier by the fact that my hands and feet were still shaking. I wiped my eyes on the rolled-up sleeve of my khaki shirt.

The clouds were gone, and I could use the stars as a heading reference, so at least we were making some kind of progress in the direction we wanted to go.

"Tell radio to send out a report," I told Amme. " 'Searchlights at Rabaul.' Have him put in everything else he can think of."

"Varitek is in no shape to send anything."

"Have Pottinger do it. Anybody who knows some Morse code can send it in plain English."

"You want to claim the cruiser?"

"Have him put in just what we saw. People saw fire. Leave it at that."

"With Mr. Modahl dead . . . it would look good if we claimed the cruiser for him."

"Do like I told you," I snapped. "A hundred cruisers won't help him now. Then come back and help me fly this pig."

Ten minutes later Amme was back. "Some flak hit the radio power supply. We can't transmit."

FIVE

When the sun rose Varitek was dead. The mountains of New Britain were sinking into the sea in our right rear quarter, and ahead were endless sun-speckled sea and open, empty sky. Right then I would have appreciated some clouds. When I next looked back, the mountains were lost in the haze.

Dutch Amme sat in the left seat and I in the right. Both of us exerted pressure on the rudder and worked to keep the *Witch* flying straight. We did that by reference to the sun, which had come up over the sea's rim more or less where we thought it should if we were flying south. As it climbed the sky, we tried to make allowances.

I also kept an eye on the set of the swells, which

seemed to show a steady wind from the southeast, a head wind. I flew across the swells at an angle and hoped this course would take us home.

Our airspeed, Amme estimated, was about 80 mph. At this speed, with a little head wind, it would take nearly seven hours to reach Namoia Bay.

Fuel was a problem. I had Amme repeat everything he had told me as we flew down the strait, only this time I listened and asked questions. The left wing had some holes in it, and we had lost gasoline. We were pouring the stuff into the right engine to stay airborne. The upshot of all this was that he thought we could stay up for maybe six hours, maybe a bit less.

"So you're saying we can't make Namoia Bay?"

Amme thrust his jaw out, eyed me belligerently. This, I had learned, was the way he dealt with authority, the world, officers. "That's right, sir. We'll be swimming before we get there."

Of course, the distance and flying time to Namoia Bay were also estimates. Still, running the *Witch* out of gas and making a forced landing in the open sea was a surefire way to die young. I knew just enough about Catalinas to know that even if we survived an open-ocean landing in this swell and were spotted from the air, no sane person would risk a plane and his life attempting to rescue us. Cats weren't designed to operate in typical Pacific rollers in the open sea.

If we couldn't make Namoia Bay, we needed a sheltered stretch of water to land on, the lee of an island or a lagoon or bay.

There were islands ahead, some big, some small, all covered with inhospitable jungle.

Then there was Buna, on the northern shore of the New Guinea peninsula.

"What about Buna?" I asked Amme and Pottinger, who was standing behind the seats. "Can we make it?"

"The Japs are still in Buna," Amme said.

"I heard they left," Pottinger replied.

"I'd hate to get there and find out you heard wrong," Amme shot back.

So much for Buna.

I had Pottinger sit in the right seat while I took a break to use the head. The interior of the plane was drafty, and when I saw the hull, I knew why. Damage was extensive, apparently from flak and the bomb blasts. Gaping holes, bent plates and stringers . . . I could look through the holes and see the sun reflecting on the ocean. The air whistling up through the wounds made the hair on the back of my head stand up. When we landed, we'd be lucky if this thing stayed above water long enough for us to get out of it. Hell, we'd be lucky if it stayed in one piece when it hit the water.

As I stood there looking at the damage, feeling the slipstream coming through the holes, I couldn't help thinking that this adventure was going to cement my reputation as a Jonah with the dive-bomber guys. They were going to put me in the park for the pigeons. Which pissed me off a little, though there wasn't a damn thing I could do about it.

Varitek's and Modahl's corpses lay in the walkway in

the center compartment. I had to walk gingerly to get around. Just seeing them hit me hard. The way it looked, this plane was going to be their coffin. Somehow that seemed appropriate. I had hopes the rest of us could do better, though I was pretty worried.

When I got back to the cockpit I stood behind Amme and Pottinger, who were doing as good a job of wrestling this flying pig southward as I had. Still, they wanted me to take over, so I climbed back in the right seat. Amme suggested the left, but I was used to using the prop and throttle controls with my left hand and the stick with my right, so figured I would be most comfortable with that arrangement.

Someone opened a box or two of C rations, and we ate ravenously. With two guys dead, you think we'd have lost our appetites, but no.

AMME:

We were in a heap of hurt. We were in a shot-up, crippled, hunk-of-junk airplane in the middle of the South Pacific, the most miserable real estate on the planet, and our pilot had never landed a seaplane in his life. Jesus! The other guys pretended that things were going to work out, but I had done the fuel figures, and I knew. We weren't going to make it, even if this ensign was God's other son.

I tried to tell the ensign and Pottinger; those two didn't seem too worried. Officers! They must get a lobotomy with their commission.

Lieutenant Modahl was the very worst. God-damned idiot. The fucking guy thought he was bulletproof and lived it that way . . . until the Japs got him. Crazy or brave, dead is dead.

The truth is we were all going to end up dead, even me, and I wasn't brave or crazy.

POTTINGER:

The crackers in the C rations nauseated me. The only gleam of hope in this whole mess was the right engine, which ran like a champ. Not enough gas, this little redheaded fool ensign for a pilot, a damaged hull . . .

Funny how a man's life can lead to a mess like this. Just two years ago I was studying Italian art at Yale . . .

Searchlights! The Japs rigged up searchlights to kill Black Cats. They probably nailed Snyder with them, and miracle of miracles, here came another victim. Those Americans!

Modahl. A braver man never wore shoe leather. I tried not to look at his face as we laid him out in back and covered him with his flight jacket.

In a few hours or days we'd all be as dead as Modahl and Varitek. I knew that, and yet, my mind refused to accept the reality. Wasn't that odd?

Or was it merely human?

"We're going to have to ditch somewhere," I told everyone on the intercom. "Everyone put on a life vest now. Break out the emergency supplies and the raft, get everything ready so when we go in the water we can get it out of the plane ASAP."

They knew what to do, they just needed someone to tell them to do it. I could handle that. After Amme got his vest on, I put on mine and hooked up the straps.

I had Pottinger bring the chart. I wanted a sheltered stretch of water to put the plane in beside an island we could survive on. And the farther from the Japs the better.

One of the Trobriand Islands. Which one would depend upon our fuel.

We were flying at about a thousand feet. Without the altimeter all I could do was look at the swells and guess. The higher we climbed, the more we could see, but if a Japanese fighter found us, our best defense was to fly just above the water to prevent him from completing firing passes.

I looked at the sun. Another two hours, I decided, then we would climb so we could see the Trobriand Islands from as far away as possible.

As we flew along I found myself thinking about Oklahoma when I was a kid, when my dad and sister and I were still living together. I couldn't remember what my mother looked like; she died when I was very young. I remembered my sister's face, though. Maybe she resembled Mama.

The island first appeared as a shadow on the horizon, just a darkening of that junction of sea and sky. I turned the plane ten degrees right to hit it dead on.

The minutes ticked away as I stared at it, wondering.

Finally I checked my watch. Five hours. We had attacked the harbor five hours earlier.

Ten minutes later I could definitely see that it was an island, a low green thing, little rise on the spine, which meant it wasn't coral.

Pottinger was in the left seat at that time, so I pointed it out to him. He merely stared, didn't say anything. About that time Dutch Amme came down from the flight engineer's station and announced that the temps were rising on the starboard engine.

"And we're running out of gas. An hour more, at the most."

I pointed out the island to him, and he had to grab the back of the seat to keep from falling.

In less than a minute we had everyone trooping up to the cockpit to take a look. Finally, I ran them all back to their stations.

That island looked like the promised land.

POTTINGER:

A miracle, that was what it was. We were delivered. We were going to make it, going to live. Going to have some tomorrows.

I didn't know whether to laugh or cry. The island was there, yet it was so far away. We would reach it, land in the lee, swim ashore . . .

Please God, let us live. Let me and these others live to marry and have children and contribute something to the world.

Hear me. Let us do this.

HOFFMAN:

I was so happy I couldn't stand still. I wanted to pound everyone on the back. Sure, I had been fighting despair, telling myself we weren't going to die when I really figured we might. The hull was a sieve—when the ensign set the *Witch* in the water we were going to have to get out as it sank. I knew that, everyone did. And still, *now* we had a chance.

"Fighter!"

One of the guys in the blisters saw it first and called it.

"A float fighter."

I rolled the trim over a bit, got us drifting downward toward the water. The elevator control cables had been damaged in the bomb blast. The trim wheel was the only reason we were still alive.

"He hasn't seen us yet. Still high, crossing from starboard to port behind us, heading nearly east it looks like."

After a bit, "Okay, he's three miles or so out to the east, going away. Never saw us."

The Japanese put some of their Zeros on floats, which made a lot of sense since the Zero had such great range. The float fighters could be operated out of bays and lagoons where airfields didn't exist and do a nice job of patrolling vast expanses of ocean. The performance penalty they paid to carry the floats was too great to allow them to go toe-to-toe with land or carrier-based fighters. They could slice and dice a Catalina, though.

"Shit, it's coming back."

I kept the Cat descending. We were a couple hundred feet above the water, far too high. I wanted us right on the wavetops.

"He's coming in from the port stern quarter, curving, coming down, about a half mile . . ."

I could hear someone sobbing on the intercom.

"I don't know who's making that goddamn noise," I said, "but it had better stop."

We were about a hundred feet high, I thought, when the float fighter opened fire. I saw his shells hit the water in front of us and heard the fifty in the port blister open up with a short burst. And another, then a long rolling blast as the plane shuddered from the impact of cannon shells.

The fighter pulled out straight ahead, so he went over us and out to my right. He flew straight until he was well out of range of our gun in the starboard blister, then initiated a gentle turn to come around behind.

"Anybody hurt?" I asked.

"He ripped the port wing, which is empty," Dutch Amme said.

"Good shooting, since he had to break off early."

I was down on the water by then, very carefully working the trim. I didn't have much altitude control remaining—if we hit the water at speed our problems would be permanently over.

I thought about turning into this guy when he committed himself to one side or the other. The island dead ahead had me paralyzed though. There it was, a strip of green between sea and sky. Instinctively, I knew that it was our only hope, and I didn't want to waste a drop of gas in my haste to get there.

Perhaps I could skid the plane a little to try to throw off the Zero pilot's aim. I fed in some rudder, twisted the yoke to hold it level.

And the lousy crate began sinking. We bounced once on a swell and that damn near did it for us right there. We lost some speed and hung right on the ragged edge of a stall. Long seconds crept by before we accelerated enough for me to exhale. By then I had the rudder where it belonged, but it was a close thing. At least the plane didn't come apart when it kissed the swell.

Pottinger was hanging on for dear life. "Don't kill us," he pleaded.

On the next pass the Zero tried to score on the starboard engine, the only one keeping us aloft. I could feel the shells slamming into us, tearing at the area just behind the cockpit. Instinctively I ducked my head, trying to make myself as small as possible.

I could hear one of the waist fifties pounding.

"Are you gunners going to shoot this guy or let him fuck us?"

With us against the water, the Zero couldn't press home his attacks, but he was hammering us good before he had to break off.

"He holed the right tank," Amme shouted. "We're losing fuel."

Oh, baby!

"He's streaming fuel or something," Hoffman screamed. "You guys hit him that last pass."

They all started talking at once. I couldn't shut them up.

"If he's crippled, the next pass will be right on the water, from dead astern," I told Pottinger. "He'll pour it to us."

"Naw. He'll head for home."

"Like hell. He'll kill us or die trying. That's what I'd do if I were him."

Sure enough, the enemy fighter came in low so he could press the attack and break off without hitting the ocean. He was directly behind, dead astern, so both the blister gunners cut loose with their fifties. Short bursts, then longer as he closed the distance.

Someone was screaming on the intercom, shouting curses at the Jap, when the intercom went dead.

I could feel the cannon shells punching home—the cannons in Zeros had low cyclic rates; I swear every round this guy fired hit us. One fifty abruptly stopped firing. The other finished with a long buzz saw burst, then the Zero swept overhead so close I could hear the roar of his engine. At that point it was running better than ours, which was missing badly.

I glanced up in time to see that the enemy fighter was trailing fire. He went into a slight left turn and gently descended until he hit the ocean about a mile from us. Just a little splash, then he was gone.

Our right engine still ran, though fuel was pouring out of the wing. As if we had any to spare.

The island lay dead ahead, but oh, too far, too far.

Now the engine began missing.

We'd never make it. Never.

Coughing, sputtering, the engine wasn't developing enough power to hold us up.

I shouted at Pottinger to hang on, but he had already let go of the controls and braced himself against the instrument panel. As I rolled the trim nose up, I gently retarded the throttle.

Just before we kissed the first swell the engine quit dead. We skipped once, I rolled the trim all the way back, pulled the yoke back even though the damn cables were severed, and the *Sea Witch* pancaked. She must have stopped dead in about ten feet. I kept traveling forward until my head hit the instrument panel, then I went out.

POTTINGER:

The ensign wasn't strapped in. In all the excitement he must have forgotten. The panel made a hell of a gash in his forehead, so he was out cold and bleeding profusely.

The airplane was settling fast. I opened the cockpit hatch and pulled him out of his seat. I couldn't have gotten him up through the hatch if Hoffman hadn't come up to the cockpit. The ensign weighed about 120, which was plenty, let me tell you. It was all Hoffman and I could do to get him through the hatch, then we hoisted ourselves through.

The top of the fuselage was just above water. It was a miracle that the Jap float fighter didn't set us on fire, and he probably would have if we had been carrying more fuel.

"What about the others?" I asked Hoffman.

"Huntington is dead. The Zero got him. So is Amme. I don't know about Tucker or Svenson."

We were about to step off the bow to stay away from the props when a wave swept us into the sea. I popped the cartridges to inflate my vest, then struggled with the ensign's. I also had to tighten the straps of his vest, then attend to mine—no one ever put those things on tightly enough. I was struggling to do all this and keep our heads above water when I felt something hit my foot.

The ensign was still bleeding, and these waters were full of sharks. A wave of panic swept over me, then my foot hit it again. Something solid. I put my foot down.

The bottom. I was standing on the bottom with just my nose out of the water.

"Hoffman! Stand up!"

We were inside the reef. A miracle. Delivered by a miracle. The ensign had gotten us just close enough.

The *Sea Witch* refused to go under, of course, because she was resting on the bottom. Her black starboard wingtip and vertical stabilizer both protruded prominently from the water.

When we realized the situation, Hoffman worked his way aft and checked on the others. He found three bodies.

We had to get ashore, so we set out across the lagoon toward the beach, walking on the bottom and pulling the ensign, who floated in his inflated life vest.

"He took a hell of a lick," I told Hoffman.

"Maybe he'll wake up," Hoffman said, leaving unspoken the other half of it, that maybe he wouldn't.

HOFFMAN:

The only thing that kept me sane was taking care of the ensign as we struggled over the reef.

Maybe he was already dead, or dying. I didn't know. I tried not to think about it. Just keep his head up.

Oh, man. I couldn't believe they were all dead—Lieutenant Modahl, Chief Amme, Swede Svenson, Tucker, Huntington, Varitek. I tried not to think about it and could think of nothing else. All those guys dead!

We were next. The three of us. There we were, castaways on a jungle island in the middle of the ocean and not another soul on earth knew. How

long could a guy stay alive? We'd be ant food before anyone ever found us. If they did.

Of course, if the Japs found us before the Americans, we wouldn't have to worry about survival.

POTTINGER:

Fighting the currents and swells washing over that uneven reef and through the lagoon while dragging the ensign was the toughest thing I ever had to do. The floor of the lagoon was uneven, with holes in it, and sometimes Hoffman and I went under and fought like hell to keep from drowning.

We must have struggled for an hour before we got to knee-deep water, and another half hour before we finally dragged the ensign and ourselves up on the beach. We lay there gasping, desperately thirsty, so exhausted we could scarcely move.

Hoffman got to his knees, finally, and looked around. The beach was a narrow strip of sand, no more than ten yards wide; the jungle began right at the high-water mark.

At his urging we crawled into the undergrowth out of sight. The ensign we dragged. He was still breathing, had a pulse, and thank God the bleeding had stopped, but he didn't look good.

The *Witch* was about a mile out on the reef. The tail stuck up prominently like an aluminum sail.

"I hope the Japs don't see that," Hoffman remarked.

"If we can't find water, it won't matter," I told

him. "We'll be praying for the Japs to come along and put us out of our misery."

After some discussion, he went one way down the beach and I went the other. We were looking for freshwater, a stream running into the sea . . . something.

At some point I became aware that I was lying in sand . . . in shade . . . in wet clothes . . . with bugs and gnats and all manner of insects eating on me.

My head was splitting, so I didn't pay much attention to the bugs, though I knew they were there.

I managed to pry my eyes open . . . and could barely make out light and darkness. I thrashed around awhile and dug at my eyes and rubbed at the bugs and passed out again.

The second time I woke up it was dark. My eyes were better, I thought, yet there was nothing to see. I could hear waves lapping nervously.

The thought that we had made it to the island hit me then. I lay there trying to remember. After a while most of the flight came back, the flak in the darkness, the Zero on floats, settling toward the water with one engine dead and the other dying . . .

I became aware that Pottinger was there beside me. He had a baby bottle in his survival vest, which he had filled with freshwater. He let me drink it. I have never tasted anything sweeter.

Then he went away, back for more I guess.

After a while I realized someone else was there. It took me several minutes to decide it was Hoffman.

"Are we the only ones alive?" I asked, finally.

"Yes," Hoffman said.

SIX

The next day, our first full day on the island, I was feeling human again, so Pottinger, Hoffman, and I went exploring. Fortunately, my head wasn't bleeding, and the headache was just that, a headache. We had solid land—okay, sand—under our feet, and we had a chance. Not much of one, but a chance. I was still wearing a pistol, and all of us had knives.

We were also hungry enough to eat a shoe.

We worked our way east along the beach, taking our time. As we walked we discussed the situation. Hoffman was for going out to the plane and trying to salvage a survival kit; Pottinger was against it. There was a line of thunderstorms off to the east and south that seemed to be coming our way. Still hours away, the storms were agitating the swells. Long, tall rollers crashed on the reef, and smaller swells swept through the lagoon.

Watching the swells roll through the shallows, I thought the wreck of the *Sea Witch* too far away and the water too dangerous. Then we saw a group of shark fins cruising along, and the whole idea of going back to the plane sort of evaporated. We certainly needed the survival kits; we were just going to have to wait for a calmer day.

I had seen the island from the air, though at a low angle, and knew it wasn't small. Trying to recall, I estimated it was eight or nine miles long and a mile wide at the widest part. Probably volcanic in origin, the center of the thing reached up a couple hundred feet or so in elevation, if my memory was correct. I remembered the little hump that I flew toward when we were down low against the sea.

The creeks running down from that rocky spine contained good water, so we wouldn't die of thirst. There was food in the sea, if we could figure out a way to get it. There were things to eat—birds and snakes and such—in the jungle, if we could catch them. All in all, I figured we could make out.

If there weren't any Japs on this island.

That was our immediate concern, so we hiked along, taking our time, looking and listening.

On the eastern end of the island the jungle petered out into an area of low scrub and sand dunes. It was getting along toward the middle of the day, so we sat to rest. After all I had been through, I could feel my own weakness, and I was sure the others could also. But sitting wasn't getting us anyplace, so we dusted our fannies and walked on.

The squall line was almost upon us when we found the first skid mark on the top of a dune.

"Darn if that furrow doesn't look like it was made by the keel of a seaplane," Hoffman said.

I took a really good look, and I had to agree.

I took out my pistol and worked the action, jacked a shell into my hand. The gun was gritty, full of sand and sea salt.

"Going to rain soon," Pottinger said, looking at the sky.

"Let's see if we can find a dry place and sit it out," I said, looking around. I spotted a clump of brush under a small stand of palms, and headed for it. The others were in no hurry, although the gray wall of rain from the storm was nearly upon us.

"Maybe it's Joe Snyder's crew, where he went down in *Charity's Sake*."

"Maybe," I admitted.

"Let's go look." If Hoffman had had a tail, he would have wagged it.

"Later."

"Hell, no matter where we hide, we're going to get wet. If it's them, they've got food, survival gear, all of that."

"Could be Japs, you know."

He was sure the Japanese didn't leave a seaplane mark.

The first gust of rain splattered us.

"I'm going to sit this one out," I said, and turned

back toward the brush I had picked out. Pottinger was right behind.

Hoffman ran up beside me. "Please, sir. Let me go on ahead for a look."

I looked at Pottinger. He was a lieutenant (junior grade), senior to me, but since I was the deputy plane commander, he hadn't attempted to exert an ounce of authority. Nor did I think he wanted to.

"No," I told Hoffman. "The risk is too great. The Japs won't want to feed us if they get their hands on us."

"They won't get me."

"No."

"You're just worried I'll tell 'em you're here."

"If they catch you, kid, it won't matter what you tell 'em. They'll come looking for us."

"Mr. Pottinger." Hoffman turned to face the jay-gee. "I appeal to you. All our gear is out in the lagoon. You know the guys in *Charity's Sake* as well as I do."

Pottinger looked at me and he looked at Hoffman and he looked at the squall line racing toward us. He was tired and hungry and had never made a life-or-death decision in his life.

"Snyder could have made it this far," he said to me.

"There's a chance," I admitted.

He bit his lip and made his decision. "Yes," he told the kid. "But be careful, for Christ's sake."

Hoffman grinned at Pottinger and scampered away just as the rain hit. I jogged over to the brush I had seen and crawled in. It wasn't much shelter. Pottinger joined me.

"It's probably Snyder," he said, more to himself than to me.

"Could be anybody."

There was a little washout under the logs. We huddled there.

"Hoffman's right about one thing," I told Pottinger. "We won't be much drier here than if we had stayed out in it."

While it rained I field-stripped the Colt and cleaned the sand and grit out of it as best I could, then put it back together and reloaded it. It wasn't much of a weapon, but it was something. I had a feeling we were going to need everything we had.

After the squall had passed, the fresh wind felt good. We sat on a log and let the wind dry us out.

We were alive, and the others were dead. So the wind played with our hair as we looked at the sea and sky with living eyes.

For how long?

I had seen much of death these last few months, had killed a few men myself . . . and oh, it was ugly. Ugly!

Anyone who thinks war is glorious has never seen a fresh corpse.

Yet we kill each other, ruthlessly, mercilessly, without qualm or remorse, all for the greater glory of our side.

Insanity. And this has been the human experience since the dawn of time.

Musing thus, I kept an eye out for Hoffman. He didn't come back. After an hour I was worried.

Pottinger was worried, too. "This isn't good," he said.

We waited another hour, a long, slow hour as the rain squall moved on out over the lagoon, and the sun came boiling through the dissipating clouds. Extraordinary how hot the tropical sun can get on bare skin.

The minutes dragged. My head thumped and my stomach tied itself into a knot. I wanted water badly.

One thing was certain; we couldn't stay put much longer. We needed to get about the business of finding drinkable water and something to eat.

"I guess I fucked that up," Pottinger said.

"Let's follow the keel mark," I suggested.

We didn't walk, we sneaked along, all bent over, even crawled through one place where the green stuff was thin. Hoffman's tracks were still visible in places, only partially obliterated by the rain. And so were the scrapes of the flying boat's keel, deep cuts in the sand where it touched, skipped, then touched again. The plane had torn the waist-high brush out of the ground everywhere it touched. Still, there was enough of it standing that it limited our visibility. And the visibility of the Japs, if there were Japs.

The thought had finally occured to Pottinger that if we could follow Hoffman, someone else could backtrack him. He was biting his lip so tightly that blood was leaking down his chin. His face was paper white.

The pistol felt good in my hand.

We had gone maybe a quarter of a mile when we saw the reflection of the sun off shiny metal. We got behind some brush and lay on the ground.

"That's no black Catalina," I whispered to Pottinger, who nodded.

Screwing up our courage, we crawled a few more yards on our hands and knees. Finally we came to the place where we could clearly see the metal, which turned out to be the twin tails of a large airplane. Japanese. The rest of the airplane appeared to be behind some trees and brush, partially out of sight.

"A Kawanishi flying boat," Pottinger whispered into my ear. "A Mavis." He was as scared as I was.

"I'm sorry," he said, his voice quavering. "You were right, and I was wrong. Letting Hoffman go running off alone was a mistake."

"Don't beat yourself up over it," I told him. "There aren't many right or wrong decisions. You make the best choice you can because the military put you there and told you to decide, then we all get on with it."

"Yeah."

"You gotta remember that none of this matters very much."

"Ahh . . ."

"You stay here. I'll go see what Hoffman's gotten himself into."

I wasn't going to go crawling over to that plane. Hoffman had probably done that. His tracks seemed to go that way. I set off at a ninety-degree angle, crawling on my belly, the pistol in my right hand.

When I'd gone at least a hundred yards, I turned to parallel the Mavis's landing track. After another hundred yards I heard voices. I froze.

They were speaking Japanese.

I lay there a bit, trying to see. The voices were demanding, imperious.

Taking my time, staying on my stomach, I crawled closer.

I heard Hoffman pleading, begging. "Don't hit me again, for Christ's sake." And a chunk of something heavy hitting flesh.

Ooh boy!

When they were finished with Hoffman, they were going to come looking for Pottinger and me. If they weren't already looking.

I had to know how many of them there were.

I crawled closer, trying to see around the roots of the grass bunches that grew on the dunes.

The Mavis had four engines, one of which was blackened and scorched. Either it caught fire in the air, or someone shot it up.

Finally I got to a place where I could see the men standing in a circle.

There were four of them. They were questioning Hoffman in Japanese. A lot of good that would do. I never met an American sailor who understood a word of it.

The Japs were taking turns beating Hoffman with a club of some kind. Clearly, they were enjoying it.

The Mavis was pretty torn up. Lots of holes, maybe fifty-caliber. It looked to me like a Wildcat or Dauntless had had its way with it.

I kept looking around, trying to see if there were any

more Japs. Try as I might, I could see only those four. Two of them had rifles though.

About then they whacked Hoffman so hard he passed out. One of them went for water, dumped it on him to bring him around. Another, decked out in an officer's uniform, went over to a little pile of stuff under a palm tree and pulled out a sword.

They were going to chop off the kid's head.

Shit!

I should never have let him go trooping off by himself.

The range was about forty yards. I steadied that pistol with a two-hand grip and aimed it at the Jap with the rifle who was facing me. I wanted him first.

I took my time. Just put that front sight on his belt buckle and squeezed 'er off like it was Tuesday morning at the range. I knocked him off his feet.

I didn't have the luxury of time with the second one. I hit him, all right, probably winged him. The other one with the rifle went to his belly and was looking around, trying to see where the shots were coming from. I only had his head and one arm to shoot at, so I took a deep breath, exhaled, and touched it off. And got him.

The officer with the sword had figured out where I was by that time and was banging at me with a pistol.

I rolled away. Got to my feet and ran, staying as low as possible, ran toward the tail of the Mavis while the officer popped off three in my direction.

"How many of them were there, Hoffman?" I roared, loud as I could shout.

"Four," he answered, then I heard another shot.

I ran the length of the flying boat's fuselage, sneaked a peek around the bow. Hoffman lay sprawled in the dirt, blood on his chest, staring fixedly at the sky.

The Jap bastard had shot him!

I sneaked back along the hull of the Mavis, thinking the guy might follow me around.

Finally, I wised up. I got down on my belly and crawled away from the Mavis.

I figured the Jap officer wanted one of those rifles as badly as I did, and that was where he'd end up. I went out about a hundred yards and got to my feet. Staying bent over as much as possible, I trotted around to where I could see the Japs I had shot.

The officer wasn't in sight. I figured he was close by anyway.

I lay down behind a clump of grass, thought about the situation, wondered what to do next.

I had just about made up my mind to crawl out of there and set up an ambush down the beach when something whacked me in the left side so hard I almost lost consciousness.

Then I heard the shot. A rifle.

With what was left of my strength, I pulled my right hand under me. Then I lay still.

I was hit damned bad. As I lay there the shock of the bullet began wearing off and the pain started way up inside me.

I tried not to breathe, not to move, not to do anything. It was easy. I could feel the legs going numb, feel the life leaking out.

For the longest time I lay there staring at the sand, trying not to blink.

I heard him, finally. Heard the footfall.

He nudged me once with the barrel of his rifle, then used his foot to turn me over.

A look of surprise registered on his face when I shot him.

POTTINGER:

I heard the shots, little pops on the wind, then silence. After a while another shot, louder, then twenty minutes or so later, one more, muffled.

After that, nothing.

Of course I had no way of knowing how many Japanese there were, what had happened, if Hoffman or the ensign were still alive . . .

I wanted desperately to know, but I couldn't make myself move. If I just sat up, I could see the tail of the Mavis . . . and they might see me.

I huddled there frozen, waiting for Hoffman and the ensign to come back. I waited until darkness fell.

Finally, I slept.

The next morning nothing moved. I could hear nothing but the wind. After a couple of hours I knew I was going to have to take a chance. I had to have food. I tried to move and found I couldn't.

Another hour passed. Then another. Ashamed of myself and nauseated with fear, I crawled.

I found them around the Japanese flying boat, all dead. The four Japanese and the two Americans. The Japanese officer was lying across the ensign.

There was food, so I ate it. The water I drank.

I put them in a row in the sand and got busy on a grave. I shouldn't have let Hoffman go exploring. I should be lying there dead instead of the ensign.

Digging helped me deal with it.

The trouble came when I had to drag them to the grave. I was crying pretty badly by then, and the ensign and Hoffman were just so much dead meat. And starting to swell up. I tried not to look at their faces . . . and didn't succeed.

I dragged the two Americans into the same hole and filled it in the best I could.

I was shaking by then, so I set to digging on a bigger hole for the Japanese. It was getting dark by the time I got the bodies in that hole and filled it and tamped it down.

The next day I inventoried the supplies in the Mavis. There was fishing gear, canned food, bottled water, pads to sleep on, blankets, an ax, matches.

After I'd been on the island about a week I decided to burn the Mavis. The fuel tanks were shot full of holes and empty, which was probably why the Mavis was lying on this godforsaken spit of sand in the endless sea.

It took two days of hard work to load the fuse-lage with driftwood. I felt good doing it, as if I were accomplishing something important. Looking back, I realize that I was probably half-crazy at that time, irrational. I ate the Japanese rations, worked on stuffing the Mavis with driftwood, watched the sky, and cried uncontrollably every now and then.

By the end of the second day I had the plane fairly full of driftwood. The next morning at dawn I built a fire in there with some Japanese matches and rice paper. The metal in the plane caught fire about an hour later and burned for most of the day. I got pretty worried that evening, afraid that I had lit an eternal flame to arouse Japanese curiosity. The fire died, finally, about midnight, though it smoldered for two more days and nights. Thank God I had been sane enough to wait for morning to light it.

With the fire finally out, I packed all the supplies I had salvaged from the Mavis and moved four miles along the south side of the island to a spot where a freshwater creek emptied into the sea. It took three trips to carry the loot.

I never did try to cross the lagoon to the wreck of the *Sea Witch*. On one of my exploratory hikes around the island a few weeks later I saw that she was gone, broken up by a storm or swept off the reef into deeper water.

I fell into a routine. Every morning I fished. I

always had something by noon, usually before, so I built a fire and cooked it and ate on it the rest of the day. During the afternoon I explored and gathered driftwood, which I piled into a huge pile. My thought was that if and when I saw a U.S. ship or plane, I would light it off as a signal fire. I had a hell of pile collected but finally ran out of matches that would light. The rain and the humidity ruined them. After that I ate my fish raw.

And so my days passed, one by one. I lost count. There was nothing on the island but the jungle and birds, and wind and rain and surf. And me. Just me and my ghosts alone on that speck of sand and jungle lost in an endless universe of sea and sky.

Later I learned that five months passed before I was rescued by the crew of a U.S. Navy patrol boat searching for a lost aircrew. Not the crew of the *Witch* or *Charity's Sake*, but a B-24 crew that had also disappeared into the vastness of the great Pacific. The war was way north and west by then.

I must have been a sight when they found me, burned a deep brown by the sun and almost naked, with only a rag around my waist. My beard and hair were wild and tangled, and I babbled incoherently.

The Navy sent me back to the States. They kept me in a naval hospital for a while until I sort of got it glued back together. Then they gave me a medical discharge.

Cut off from human contact during those long

nights and long, long days on that island, I could never get the ensign and Modahl and the other guys from the *Witch* out of my mind. They have been with me every day of my life since.

I have never figured out why they died and I lived.

To this day I still don't know. It wasn't because I was a better person or a better warrior. They were the warriors—they carried me. They had courage, I didn't. They had faith in each other and themselves, and I didn't. Why was it that they died and I was spared?

The old Vikings would have said that Modahl and the ensign were the lucky ones.

In the years that have passed since I flew in the *Sea Witch* the world has continued to turn, the seasons have come and gone, babies have been born and old people have passed away. The earth continues as before.

As I get older I have learned that the ensign spoke the truth: The fate of individuals matters very little. We are dust on the wind.

The 17th Day

"What's a Yank doing in the bleedin' RFC anyway, I'd like to know," Nigel Cook asked between slurps of tea. "As if the bleedin' RFC didn't have troubles enough, eh, with the Diggers and Canucks and provincials from all over. Wouldn't the Frogs take you for that Lafayette outfit?"

Paul Hyde had had more than enough of Nigel Cook the last two weeks. Two weeks and two days. Sixteen days of fun and games since he'd reported to the squadron in France. "I don't speak Frog," he muttered at Cook, because he had to say something. After all, Cook was the squadron pilot with the most service-time at the front.

Cook thought Hyde's retort screamingly funny. He elbowed the pilot next to him at the breakfast table and giggled soundlessly. Finally he regained control of himself and managed, "Doesn't speak Frog." Then he succumbed to another silent giggling fit.

"Looks like ol' Cook's nerves are about shot," Robert MacDonald murmured to Hyde.

"Has he really been in the squadron a whole year?"

"A week short. He should go home any day now."

Hyde chewed his toast mechanically, sipped at strong, black tea. Down the table, Cook was pouring brandy into his tea and still giggling. He wiped tears from his eyes, managed to get a cigarette going.

"They ought to have sent him home months ago," Hyde whispered to MacDonald.

"No doubt, Tex, old man. No doubt." The Brits all called Hyde "Tex," although he was from Boston and had never been west of the Hudson. Mac motored on: "Cook isn't much good to us now, I'm afraid. Has the wind up rather badly."

Having the wind up was an occupational hazard, Hyde had learned. He grunted in reply.

"But we've got you and those two virgins who arrived yesterday, so we'll give the ol' Hun a bloody good go today, eh?"

"Yeah."

"Today you go over the hump, I believe."

"Today is my seventeenth day," Hyde acknowledged, and finished up the last of his toast. Seventeen days was the average life expectancy of a British aviator at the front, according to army statistics compiled during the grim days of 1915 and 1916.

"We've got better machines now, thank God," Mac said cheerfully. He had two months at the front under his belt and liked to play the role of veteran warrior. "If a chap learns the trade, stays fit and reasonably sober, snipes his Huns only after a careful look all about, why, I think he could grow old and gray in this business. It's the new men getting potted who ruin the averages."

"Quite so," said Paul Hyde. He had fallen in love with these meaningless little phrases of conversational British and salted them around at every opportunity.

"After all, the average was made up of a few old birds who'd grown positively senile and a lot of young ducks who couldn't see a Hun until he opened fire."

"So they say."

"Why, some of the new fools they send us these days get potted on their very first snipe."

"Not very cricket, that," Hyde said, as British as he could.

"Enough philosophy." Robert MacDonald slapped the table. "They tell me you're going up with me this morning. Keep your eyes peeled, don't go swanning off on your own. We've got a push on and the Huns will be quite curious. The old man will be most unhappy if I come back without you."

"I should hope."

"Let's not be overly keen, Tex. Not good form. Watch for Huns, obey my signals, don't get the wind up."

"Righto," said Paul Hyde. As he left the table he saw Nigel Cook nipping brandy straight from the flask.

Rain had fallen the previous night. In the hour before

dawn the cool, invigorating June air had a tangible substance and a pungent, earthy scent. Dew covered everything. Wisps of fog drifted through the circles of light.

"Bugger fog," Mac said.

"Getting down through this stuff will be a little chancy, don't you think, Mac?"

"The general staff isn't going to call off the war. Might as well do our bit for the king, hadn't we? Maybe this lot will burn off by the time we come back to land."

"I was wondering about the getting off. Perhaps we should get off separately, then get together on top. What do you think, Mac?"

"Quite sound, that. I'll go first, of course."

They walked to the planes, which were already parked in the takeoff position.

The sky in the east was turning pink when Paul Hyde completed his preflight inspection. The mechanics seemed quite proud of the bullet-hole patches they had completed overnight. Hyde mouthed a compliment, fastened the collar of his leather flying coat tightly, and automatically held his hand a few inches from the exhaust pipe, which ran along each side of the cockpit and ended just behind it. The pipe was cool this morning, of course, but Hyde always checked. He put his left foot in the stirrup on the fuselage and swung his right leg into the cockpit, as if he were mounting a horse. When that exhaust pipe was hot, getting in or out of an S.E.5 was a task for a careful man. Hyde's first burn, on the inside of his left thigh, was still tender.

Seated, strapped in, Hyde looked around carefully in

the predawn gloom. The glow of a nearby light mounted on a pole behind him helped.

The S.E.5A had two guns, an air-cooled Lewis on a Foster mount on the top wing, which fired over the propeller arc, and a synchronized water-cooled Vickers mounted in front of the pilot, slightly to the left of the aircraft's centerline. The Lewis used a 97-round drum that mounted on top of the weapon, the Vickers was belt-fed. Both guns were .303 caliber.

The Lewis was an anachronism, mounted above the top wing in the S.E.5A because it rode there in the Nieuport-17, a rotary-engined scout now obsolete. At the full forward position on the Foster mount, the gun fired above the prop arc along the axis of the aircraft. To clear a jam or change the drum, the pilot pulled the gun backwards and down on the mount. Flying the plane with his knees and fighting the 100-mph slipstream, he cleared the jam or wrested the empty drum off and replaced it with a full one. While still in the retracted position, the weapon could be swiveled through a limited arc and fired upward into the unprotected belly of another aircraft.

Sitting in the pilot's seat, Hyde checked the circular drum magazine of the Lewis, made sure the cocking mechanism was lubricated and moved easily, made sure the trigger cable was properly rigged, and pushed the gun forward on the circular mount until it latched. An extra drum was carried in a case above the instrument panel.

Then he turned his attention to the fixed Vickers, which was much easier to reach. The Vickers was dependent upon the proper functioning of the Constantinesco synchronization gear. If the hydraulic gear developed a leak that hand pumping couldn't overcome, the weapon was useless.

The cockpit in which he sat had been modified by the squadron. The armored seat had been removed and a wooden bench installed that allowed the pilot to sit much lower in the cockpit. The original huge windscreen was gone; in its place on this particular machine was a small, flat piece of glass that deflected the slipstream over the pilot's head.

One of the mechanics leaned in and shone an electric torch on the instrument panel. Hyde studied the levers, dials, and switches in front of him. On the seventeenth day, they seemed like old friends. Mounted on the panel were an airspeed indicator, altimeter, compass, tachometer, switch and booster mag, and petrol shutoff. Gauges informed him of oil and air pressure and the temperature of the radiator coolant.

The mixture and throttle controls were on the right side of the panel. For reasons no one could explain, they worked exactly opposite of each other. The throttle lever was full forward for full throttle, but full rich required that the mixture control be all the way aft.

A fuel pump was on the left of the panel, and a hand pump for the synchronization gear was between his knees.

The control stick had a ring mounted vertically on the top of it, hence its nickname of "spade handle." In the center on the ring were two toggle switches, one for each machine gun.

Hyde thanked the mech, who moved away. Hyde didn't need the light; he knew where everything was.

He turned on the petrol, made sure the switch and booster mag were off.

"Gas on, mag off," he called.

The linesman took the prop and moved it back and forth several times. Finally fuel began running out of the carburetor.

"Contact," the linesman called.

"Contact," Hyde echoed and turned on the mag switch.

The linesman seized the prop and gave it a mighty heave. As he did, Hyde rotated the booster mag handle and the engine started with a gentle rumble. It ticked over nicely at 500 RPM, the tach needle barely twitching at the bottom of its range.

The 200-HP liquid-cooled Hispano-Suiza engine took a while to warm up. On Hyde's right the linesmen were trying to get Mac's engine started. They pulled it through repeatedly.

Hyde settled himself into his seat, stirred the controls around, and visually checked the ailerons, elevator, and rudder. All okay.

The Hisso rumbling sweetly in the false dawn. The fog stirred by the spinning propeller, the smell of the earth, the waiting sky, life pungent and rich and mysterious— Paul Hyde had dropped out of college for this. Took a train to Montreal and joined the Canadian armed forces. In England he had wrangled a transfer to the Royal Flying Corps, which was looking for volunteers for pilot training. The whole thing was a grand adventure, or so he had assured himself at least a thousand times. Friends had died in accidents, some before his eyes, and the Germans had killed both the young pilots who'd accompanied him to France just weeks ago.

An adventure . . . the word stuck in his throat now. If by some miracle he lived through this . . .

The truth was, he probably wouldn't. Hyde knew that, and yet . . .

The best way was to take it a day at a time. Live through Day One, Day Two, etc. He was up to Day Seventeen now. If he made it through today, he had beaten the odds. If he made it through today—who knows?—he just might pull it off, live through the whole obscene bloody mess. Well, there was a chance, anyway. But first, make it through today.

The radiator thermometer indicated that the engine was warming nicely. In the cool, saturated morning air a thin ribbon of cloud developed at the tips of the slowly swinging prop and swirled back around the fuselage of the plane. The windsock hung limp.

To Hyde's dismay, as the dawn progressed, the fog seemed to be thickening.

Mac's engine was not going to start anytime soon. The sweating mechanics pulled it through a dozen times while Nigel Cook and one of the new puppies charged into the fog and got airborne. Finally Mac climbed from the cockpit in disgust and threw his leather flying helmet on the ground. He stomped over to Hyde's plane, leaned in to make himself heard.

"Bloody Frog motor won't start. Take a few minutes

to set right, the fitters say. You go on and I'll meet you in our sector."

Hyde nodded.

"Wish we still had our Nieuports," Mac added savagely.

Hyde didn't share that opinion. The squadron had reequipped with the new S.E.5A's only two weeks before Hyde arrived, and in truth, the S.E. was a better plane in every way—faster, easier to fly, more maneuverable, with two guns. . . . The only weak point was the S.E.'s geared French engine. The Hissos were temperamental. Worse, the metallurgy was substandard and quality control poor.

Now the linesmen waved Hyde off, so with his right hand he fed in throttle as he enriched the mixture and with his left he shoved the spade handle stick forward. The S.E. began to roll. Almost immediately the tail came up. Flames twinkled from the exhaust pipes on both sides of the plane and illuminated the underside of the top wings with a ghostly yellow glare.

There, tail up, accelerating, bumping along over the uneven grass as the engine's song rose to a promising growl, not too loud. The prop turned so slowly on takeoff— only 1,500 RPM—that almost no right rudder was required.

After a bit over three hundred feet of run, Paul Hyde gave a gentle tug on the stick and the nose came off the ground.

He concentrated fiercely on flying the plane. If he lost contact with the earth or the dawn in this poor visibility, he was a dead man. And if the engine stopped for any reason—he had mentally prepared himself—he was landing straight ahead regardless. Just last week an old dog died trying to turn back to the field with the motor popping, barely turning over.

When he was safely above the fog layer, Paul Hyde looked back into the gloom. And saw nothing: The field had disappeared.

The dawn's glow would be his reference this morning, for the compass was impossible to read in the dark cockpit. Hyde flew north, parallel to the trenches, with the dawn off his right wing as he climbed.

Mainly he looked for other aircraft, but he also scanned the gauzy sea below for landmarks. Here and there were towering pillars of cumulus cloud, monsters half hidden amid the patchy stratus. Hyde steered around these. In the east the sky was yellow and gold—in just moments the sun would appear.

German observation planes would be along when the light improved. Hyde's mission was to prevent German crews from photographing the front, and, if possible, to shoot them down. The job sounded straightforward enough, but it wasn't. When they weren't taking pictures, German observers could give a good account of themselves with machine guns. And there were often enemy scouts perched above the two-seaters, ready to pounce on any British mice attracted to the cheese.

This morning the air was dead calm, without a bounce or burble of any kind. The engine ran sweetly and the ship obeyed Hyde's every whim. The slightest twitch of the stick or rudders brought forth a gentle response.

Hyde charged each gun and fired a short burst. Everything was ready.

The plane swam upward past various layers of pink and gold patchy cloud, turning gently from time to time to avoid the cumulus buildups. Swatches of open sky were visible to the north and east.

The eastern sky drew Hyde's attention. It was quite bright now as the rising sun chased away the night.

Hyde was searching for specks, little black specks in the bright sky that moved slowly this way and that. Those specks would be airplanes.

Finally he remembered to search the gloom in all the other directions. The Huns could be anywhere.

The altimeter recorded his upward progress. After about sixteen minutes of flight he passed fourteen thousand feet. Further progress upward would be much slower. Hyde wanted to be as high as possible, so he kept climbing.

Below he could occasionally catch a glimpse of the ground. Once he saw the ugly brown smear of trenches.

He was near Grommecourt, he thought, but nothing was certain. He couldn't see enough of the earth to be sure. He must be careful this morning not to let the wind that must be at altitude push him too deep behind enemy lines.

He swung west, let the ship climb into the prevailing westerlies. There was enough light to easily see the altimeter now, which was moving very slowly upward. The temperature in the radiator was rising, so Hyde opened the radiator shutters to let more air through. Up, up, up as the minutes ticked past and the engine hummed sweetly. He leaned the fuel/air mixture, tightened his collar against the cold.

He was breathing shallowly now, and rapidly. The air here was thin. He must make no sudden movements, make no serious demands upon his body or his body would rebel from the lack of oxygen.

At seventeen thousand feet he let the nose come down a degree or two. The plane was slow, sluggish on the controls, and he was a touch light-headed.

He let the left wing drop a few degrees, let the nose track slowly around the horizon until he was again flying east. The sun was up now, filling the eastern sky. All the clouds were below him.

God, it was cold up here! He checked his watch. He had been airborne for forty minutes.

He put his hand over the sun, looked left and right, above and below. Out to the left, the right, behind, below, even above. His eyes never stopped moving.

Another quarter hour passed. The day was fully here, the sun a brilliant orb climbing the sky.

There, a speck against a cloud. No, two. Two specks. To his left and down a thousand feet or so.

He turned in that direction.

Definitely two planes. Flying south. Hyde was approaching them from their right front quarter, so he turned almost north, let them go past at about a mile, hoping they didn't see him. As the specks passed behind his right wing, he turned toward them and lowered the nose a tad.

Two. One alone would have been more than enough, but Hyde wasn't going to let the Hun strut about unmolested just because he had brought a friend.

At least there were no enemy scouts above. He looked carefully and saw only empty sky.

He was going fast now, the wires keening, the motor thundering again at full cry, coming down in the right rear quarter of those two planes. The distance closed nicely.

He fingered the trigger levers inside the round stick handle.

The victims flew on straight, seemingly oblivious to his ambush.

At three hundred yards he realized what they were: S.E.5's.

He turned to cross behind them. If the pilots had seen him, they gave no indication.

Perhaps he should have flown alongside, waved. But they would rag him in the mess, say that he thought they were Germans and had come to pot them. All of which would be true and hard to laugh off, so he turned behind them to sneak away.

He kept the turn in.

There! Just off the nose! A plane coming in almost head-on.

He was so surprised he forgot to do anything.

The enemy pilot shot across almost in front of him, a Fokker D-VII, with a yellow nose and a black Maltese cross on the fuselage behind the pilot.

Hyde slammed the right wing down, pulled the nose around, used the speed that he still had to come hard around in the high thin air. Unfortunately the S.E. turned slowest to the right—maybe he should have turned left.

When he got straightened out he was too far behind the Fokker to shoot.

The enemy pilot roared in after the pair of S.E.'s.

If only he had been more alert! He could have taken a shot as the enemy scout crossed his nose. Damnation!

Now the Hun swooped in on the left-most S.E. A slender feather of white smoke poured aft from the German's nose—he was shooting.

The S.E.5 seemed to stagger, the wings waggled, then the left wing dropped in a hard turn.

The Fokker closed relentlessly, its gun going.

The S.E. went over on its back and the Fokker swerved just enough to miss it, then lowered its nose even more and dove away.

Paul Hyde kept his nose down, the engine full on.

Out of the corner of his eye he saw the S.E.'s nose drop until it was going almost straight down. It couldn't do that long, he knew, or the wings would come off when the speed got too great.

He checked the Hun, going for a cloud.

Brass. The enemy pilot had brass.

But Hyde was overtaking.

He looked again for the stricken S.E., and couldn't find it.

Only now did the possibility of another Hun following the first occur to him. Guiltily he looked aft, cleared his tail. Nothing. The sky seemed empty.

He was two hundred yards behind the Fokker now, closing slowly, but closing.

The Fokker was going for a cloud.

Suddenly Paul Hyde knew how it was going to be. He was going to get a shot before the enemy pilot reached the safety of the cloud. He moved his thumb over the firing levers, looked through the post and ring sight mounted on the cowling in front of him. The enemy plane was getting larger and larger.

Without warning the nose of the enemy plane rose sharply, up, up, up.

Hyde automatically pulled hard on the stick. He was going too fast, knew he couldn't follow the Fokker into the loop, so he pulled the nose up hard and jabbed the triggers. Both guns hammered out a burst and the Fokker climbed straight up through it.

Then Hyde was flashing past, going for the cloud. He jammed the nose down just as the cloud swallowed him.

He throttled back, raised the nose until the altimeter stopped unwinding.

The S.E.5A had no attitude instruments whatsoever. All Hyde could do was hold the stick and rudder frozen, wait until his plane flew through the cloud to the other side.

His airspeed was dropping. He could feel the controls growing sloppy. He eased the nose forward a tad. The altimeter began unwinding.

God, he was high, still above thirteen thousand feet. The altimeter was going down too fast, his speed building relentlessly.

He pulled back on the stick. To no avail. The altimeter continued to fall. He was in a graveyard spiral, but whether to the right or left he could not tell.

Panic seized Paul Hyde. He tightened the pressure on the stick, pulled it back farther and farther.

No. No! Too much of this and he would tear the wings off.

He had no way of knowing if he was turning left or right. He could guess, of course, and try to right the plane with the stick. If he guessed wrong he would put the S.E. over on its back, the nose would come down, and the plane would accelerate until it shed its wings. If he guessed right, he could indeed bring the plane upright, or nearly so, but it would do him no good unless he could keep it upright in balanced flight—and he had no means to accomplish that feat. All this Hyde knew, so he fought the temptation to move the stick sideways. What he did do was pull back even harder, tighten the turn, increase the G-load.

Oh, God! Help me! Help me, please!

Something gave. He felt it break with a jolt that reached him through the seat, heard a sharp sound audible even above the engine noise.

Eleven thousand feet.

He kept back pressure on the stick. Instinct required that he do *something*, and he sensed that if he relaxed back pressure, the plane would accelerate out of control.

Ten thousand.

Fabric flapping caught his eye. A strip of fabric was peeling from the underside of the left wing. He looked, and watched the wind peel the strip the width of the wing.

Nine thousand.

Before his eyes one of the wing bracing wires failed, broke cleanly in two.

Eight.

Another jolt through the seat. Wooden wing compression ribs or longerons or something was breaking under the stress. If a wing spar went, he was a dead man.

Seven.

Hyde was having trouble seeing. The G was graying him out. He shook his head, fought against the G-forces, screamed at the top of his lungs, although he wasn't aware he was screaming.

Six . . .

Five . . .

Four . . .

And then in an eye-blink he was out of the cloud, spiraling tightly to the left. The ground was several thousand feet below. He raised the left wing, gently lifted the nose. He was so frightened he couldn't think.

Below he saw farmland. Squares of green, trees, roads, carts, horses. . . .

Was he east or west of the trenches? *Think, man, think.*

He was so cold, so scared he wanted to vomit.

A sunbeam caught his eye. He turned to place the

sun on his tail, checked the compass. It was swimming round and round, useless.

At least two lift wires were broken, a wide strip of fabric flapped behind the upper wing, one of the struts was splintered, and the damn plane flew sideways. Not a lot, but noticeably so. Hyde used right rudder and left stick to keep it level and going west.

Up ahead, the trenches. Clouds of mud and smoke . . . artillery!

The artillery emplacements were impossible to avoid. The guns roared almost in his ear. If a shell hit him, he would never know it; he would be instantly launched into eternity.

He hunched his shoulders as if he were caught in a cloudburst, waited with nerves taut as steel for the inevitable.

Then, miraculously, he was past the artillery and out over the trenches, jagged tears in a muddy brown landscape. He saw infantrymen swing their rifles up, saw the flash of the muzzle blasts, felt the tiny jolts of bullets striking the plane. No-man's-land lay beyond, torn by artillery shells which seemed to be landing randomly. The land was covered with men, British soldiers. Hyde weaved his way through the erupting fistulas of smoke and earth while he waited for a chance shell to smash him from the sky. After a lifetime he flew clear.

He recognized where he was. The airfield was just ten miles southwest.

He sweated every mile. Once he thought he felt another jolt of something breaking.

At least the fog had burned off a bit. Visibility was up to perhaps three miles.

When he saw the hangars and tents of the aerodrome, a wave of relief swept over him. With the sun shining over his shoulder onto the instrument panel, Paul Hyde eased the throttle and let the S.E. settle onto the ground. It bounced once. When it touched the second time he pulled the tail skid down into the dirt. When the plane slowed to taxi speed he used the rudder to turn the steerable tail skid, and taxied over in front of the maintenance hangar.

He was unstrapping, getting ready to climb from the cockpit, when three more bracing wires on the left side snapped and both the left wings sagged toward the ground.

A maintenance wallah came trotting up as Hyde pulled off his leather helmet and wiped the sweat from his face and hair.

From twenty feet away the damage was obvious: A strip of fabric was peeled from the lower right wing, too, one of the bracing wires for the tail was broken, at least one of the fuselage stringers behind the cockpit had snapped, the tip of the lower left wing hung only inches above the grass, the plane was peppered with several dozen bullet holes that he had picked up flying over the trenches.

The horrified M.O. didn't say anything, merely stood and looked with a forlorn expression on his face.

Hyde didn't care. He was still alive! That was something grand and exciting in a subtly glorious way.

He turned and walked across the field toward the mess. He desperately needed a drink of water.

"Rough go, old chap," the major said, eyeing the broken S.E. out the window as the mechanics towed it off the field with a lorry. "What happened?"

Hyde explained. "Went out of control in the cloud," he finished lamely.

"Albert Ball died like that, or so I've heard," the major said. He ran his fingers through his hair and looked at Hyde carefully. "Are you fit?"

"I suppose," Hyde said, taking a deep breath and setting his jaw just so. He didn't want the major to think he had the wind up.

"There's a push on, I needn't tell you. Going to have to send you up again. We've got to do our bit."

"Where's Mac?"

"He got off just a few minutes ago. If you hurry you can catch him in this sector here." The major showed him on the wall chart.

"I got a short burst into a D-VII just west of the Hun trenches."

"Plucky lad you are, Tex. If someone reports one going down, I'll let you know. Now off with you."

The next machine was older and had seen more rough service than the one he had just bent. The engine didn't seem to have the vigor it should have.

Paul Hyde coaxed it into the air and turned south. He was passing through five thousand when the engine popped a few times, then windmilled for a second or so before it resumed firing. He pulled the mixture lever full out and frantically worked the fuel pump handle.

Perhaps he should go back.

But no. The major would think . . .

The engine ran steadily enough now. Perhaps there was just a bit of dirt in the carb, maybe a slug of water in the petrol.

On he climbed, up into the morning.

He saw the German two-seater when he was still several thousand feet below it. He had been airborne about an hour and had seen a handful of British machines and several German kites, but they were too far away to stalk. This LVG was weaving around cloud towers at about twelve thousand feet. Hyde let it go over him, then turned to stalk it as he climbed.

Idly he wondered if that burst he had fired at the German scout earlier this morning had done any damage. Or if it had even struck the Fokker.

No way of knowing, of course.

In the past sixteen days he had destroyed two German machines. The first, a two-seater, he'd riddled before the observer finally slumped over.

Not willing to break off to change the Lewis drum, he'd closed to point-blank range and shot the pilot with the Vickers. The machine went out of control and eventually shed its wings. Before he died the observer put forty-two holes in Hyde's S.E.

"As a general rule," Mac had commented as he looked over the plane when Hyde returned, "it's not conducive to longevity to let the Huns shoot you about. Sooner or later the blokes are bound to hit something vital. Perhaps you should get under them and shoot upward into their belly. S.E.'s are very good in that regard."

"I was trying to do that."

Mac pretended that he hadn't heard. "Shoot the other fellow, Tex," he advised, "while avoiding getting shot oneself. That's my motto."

Hyde's second kill was a Fokker scout. Hyde didn't even realize he had fired a killing shot. He got in a burst as the Fokker dove away after riddling Hyde's leader, who fell in flames. Apparently Hyde's burst hit the German pilot, who crashed amid the British artillery behind the trenches. By the time the Tommies got to him he had bled to death.

It was all very strange, this game of kill or be killed played among the clouds. And here he was playing it again.

The two-seater this morning was looking for him. The pilot was dropping one wing, then the other, as the two men scanned the sky below. Hyde turned away, put a towering buildup between the two planes as he continued to work his way higher into the atmosphere. The air was bumpy now as the sun heated the earth and it in turn heated the atmosphere. At least the fog was gone. Visibility was six or eight miles here.

He got a glimpse of the LVG through a gap in the cloud. It was still going in the right direction, about five hundred feet above him.

When next he saw it, he was at an equal altitude but

the Hun was turning. Hyde banked sharply and kept climbing. If possible he would get well above it, then dive and overtake it, settling in beneath to spray it with the Lewis. The Brits assured him this was the best and safest way to kill two-seaters.

The Hun had turned again when next it loomed into view amid the cloud towers. It was close, within a quarter mile, and slightly below his altitude. He could see the heads of the crew. Fortunately they were looking in the opposite direction.

Hyde scanned the sky to see what had attracted the Germans' attention.

Ah-ha. An S.E. swanning closer. That might be Mac. Good old Mac!

Paul Hyde turned toward the LVG, pushed the nose forward into a gentle dive. His thumb was poised over the trigger levers.

He came in from the left stern quarter, closing rapidly. With the Hun filling the sight ring, he opened fire with both guns.

The Vickers spit five or six bullets out before it stopped abruptly. In less than a second the Lewis also ceased firing.

Holy damn! He backed off the throttle to stop his relative motion toward the enemy.

He tugged at the bolt of the Vickers. The damn thing was jammed solid. He hammered at it with his hand.

Now the observer began shooting at him. Streaks of tracer went just over the cockpit.

Cursing aloud, Hyde turned away.

He tried to get the Lewis gun to come backwards on the Foster mount. No. The damn thing was stuck!

Cursing, Hyde unfastened his seat belt, grasped the stick between his knees, and eyed the German, who was a quarter mile away now. The pilot stood up in the cockpit and used both hands to tug at the charging lever. The windblast was terrific, but he was a strong young man.

The Lewis was also jammed good. Old, inferior, shoddy ammo! What a way to fight a war!

Perhaps he could get at the bolt better if he took off the magazine drum. He pulled at the spring-loaded catch, tugged fiercely at the drum. It was jammed, too.

He was working frantically to free the drum when he realized the plane was going over on its back. The right wing was pointing at the earth.

His lower body fell from the cockpit. He latched onto the ammo drum with a death grip. His back was to the prop, his feet pointed toward the earth.

If the damned drum comes loose now . . .

The rat-tat-tat of a machine gun cut into his consciousness. Hyde heard it, but he had more pressing problems. If he fell forward into the prop, the damn thing would cut him in half.

He tried to curl his lower body back toward the cockpit. The windblast helped. He had his left foot in and his right almost there when the nose of the plane dipped toward the earth. The S.E. was going into an inverted dive.

He was screaming again, a scream of pure terror. He

was still screaming when the plane passed the vertical and he got both feet inside the cockpit combing. Still screaming when the force of gravity took over and threw him back into the cockpit like a sack of potatoes thrown into a barrel. Still screaming as he pulled the plane out of its dive and looked about wildly for the Hun two-seater, which was far above and flying away.

He lowered the nose, let the plane dive as he struggled to get his seat belt refastened.

Praise God, he was still alive.

Still alive!

Just then the engine cut out.

"It's these bloody cartridges, sir. All swelled up from moisture." The mechanic, Thatcher, displayed three of the offending brass cylinders in the palm of his hand. "They jammed the gun and the drum."

"Uh-huh."

"Bad cartridges."

"And a dud engine. The damned thing cut in and out on me all the way home. It's junk. I'm up there risking my neck in a plane with a junk motor that runs only when it wants to. The bloody RFC has to do better, Thatcher."

"We're working on it, sir," the mech said contritely. He was used to carrying the ills of the world on his thin shoulders. "But what I don't understand, Mr. Hyde," he continued, "is how you acquired two bullet holes through the pilot's seat. Came right through the bottom of the plane and up through the seat. Or vice versa. Don't see how those two bullets missed you."

"It's quite simple, Thatcher," Paul Hyde said softly. "Perfectly logical. Obviously I wasn't sitting in the seat when the bullets went sailing through."

Without further explanation he walked toward the mess tent for lunch.

Mac was already there. "I heard you've had an exciting morning, Tex."

"Much more excitement and my heart is going to stop dead."

"Oh, I doubt it. Heart attacks are rather rare in this part of France." Mac sipped a glass of red wine. "Lead poisoning and immolation seem much more prevalent."

Hyde grunted. The wine looked tempting. One glass wouldn't hurt, would it?

"You remember the new man, Cotswold-Smith? Reported last night and sat in that chair right there for breakfast? Hun shot him off Nigel's wing this morning."

Hyde helped himself to the pudding as the dish came by. "Too bad," he said politely. He didn't have any juice left to squander on Cotswold-Smith.

"Nigel says you came galloping to the rescue, chased the bleedin' Hun off."

"Little late," Hyde remarked, and tasted the pudding.

"Not your fault, of course. Did the best you could. Can't blame yourself, old man."

"Oh, shut up, Mac."

"It's these new lads that ruin the average," Mac mused.

"Don't know how to take care of themselves in the air. Disheartening, that."

The major wanted him to fly after lunch, but the plane was dud. Paul Hyde went to the little farmhouse room he shared with Mac and collapsed into his bed fully dressed. He was so tired. . . .

He couldn't sleep. The adventures of the morning were too fresh. To get so close to death and somehow survive seared each subsequent moment on the brain. The way people moved, every word they said, the way something looked, all of it took on enormous significance.

His hands still trembled from this morning.

The worst moment was when the plane rolled over with him hanging onto the Lewis drum. If that thing had come off . . .

Well, he would have had a long fall.

He lay in bed listening to the hum of engines and the noises of the enlisted men banging on machinery and wondered how it would have felt, falling, falling, falling, down toward the waiting earth and certain death.

He was dangling from the ammo drum, nothing but clouds and haze below his shoetops and his fingers slipping, when someone shook him.

"Mr. Hyde, sir! Mr. Hyde! They want you in Ops." The batman didn't leave until Hyde had his feet on the floor.

Four-thirty in the afternoon. He had been asleep

almost three hours. He splashed some water on his face, then left the room and closed the door behind him.

Three pilots stood in front of the major's desk: Mac-Donald, Cook, and one of the new men, Fitzgerald or Fitzhugh or something like that. Hyde joined them.

"HQ wants us to attack the enemy troops advancing to reinforce their line," the major explained. "Nigel, you'll lead." He stepped over to the wall chart and pointed out the roads he wanted the planes to hit.

MacDonald's face was white when he stepped from the room into the daylight. "There must be two divisions on those roads marching for the front," he whispered to Paul Hyde. "I saw them earlier this afternoon. The roads are black with them. This is murder."

"I wouldn't quite call it that," Hyde replied. "The damned Huns will be shooting back with a great deal of vigor."

"The bloody Huns are going to murder *us*. We don't stand a chance." Sweat ran down Mac's face. "God, I'm sick of this," he muttered.

"Maybe we'll get lucky," Fitzgerald said. He was right behind the two.

"I've used up all my luck," Nigel Cook said dryly. He had followed Fitzgerald through the door. "Come on, lads. Nobody lives forever. Let's go kill some bloody Huns."

Hyde snorted. Cook could act a good show on occasion. "This morning, Nigel, did you see that Fokker before he gunned Cotswold-Smith?"

Nigel Cook's face froze. His eyes flicked in Hyde's direction, then he looked forward. He walked stiffly toward the planes, which the mechanics had already started.

"Why did you ask him that?" Mac demanded.

"Everybody's a damned hero."

"You bloody fool," Mac thundered. "Nothing is going to bring that puppy back. You hear? Nothing! Cook has to live with it. Don't you understand anything?"

Mac stalked away, the new man trailing along uncertainly in his wake.

Hyde glanced at his watch. He had a few minutes. He sat down on the bench by the door of the Ops hut and lit a cigarette. The smoke tasted delicious.

One more hop today. If he lived through that, the seventeenth day was history. He had beaten the odds. Tomorrow he could worry about tomorrow.

Filthy Huns. This next little go was going to be bad. The S.E.'s were going to be ducks in the shooting gallery.

He would live or he wouldn't. That was the truth of it.

He remembered his family, his parents and his sister. As he puffed on the cigarette he recalled how they looked, what they said the last time he saw them.

His hands were still trembling.

Nigel Cook led them across the lines at fifty feet. Hyde was on Cook's wing, the new man on Mac's. The plan was for Cook and Hyde to shoot up everything on the left side of the road, Mac and Fitz to shoot up the right. When the Lewis drum was empty, they would climb and change ammo drums, then select another road.

Each plane had four bombs under the wings that the pilot could release by pulling on a wire. With a lot of practice, a man might get so he could drop the things accurately, but to do it at two hundred feet with a hundred bullets a second coming your way was more than most men had in them. Hyde hated the things. If a bullet hit one as it hung on your wing, it would blow the wing in half. He planned to drop his at the very first opportunity, and whispered to the new man to do likewise.

Fitzwater his name was, or something like that. He looked pasty when Hyde shook his hand and wished him luck.

Hyde's plane this evening was running well. Motor seemed tight, the controls well-rigged, the guns properly cleaned and lubricated.

What else is there?

"The M.O. asked that you try to bring this bus back more or less intact, Mr. Hyde," the linesman said saucily. "He said you've been using them up rather freely of late."

Hyde didn't even bother to answer that blather.

Flashes from the German trenches—the scummy people were already popping away. . . .

The clouds were lower and darker than they had been this morning. Perhaps it would rain tonight.

The four S.E.'s crossed above the trenches and headed for a supply depot that the major had marked on the map.

A bullet shattered the altimeter on the panel. Slivers

from the glass face stuck in the glove of Hyde's left hand. He used his right to brush and pull the slivers out. Specks of blood appeared on the glove.

Several lorries ahead, some tents and boxes piled about. That must be the dump. Hyde gripped the bomb release wire. Cook and the others were shooting at the lorries, but Hyde didn't bother. He flew directly toward the dump and toggled the bombs off. He checked to ensure they had fallen off the racks, but he didn't look back to see where they hit. He didn't care.

Tiny jolts came to him through the seat and stick. Those were bullets striking the aircraft, bullets fired by the men he saw just a few feet below the plane blazing away with rifles.

Fortunately most of the airplane was fabric and offered little resistance to steel projectiles. The frame was wood, however, and bullets would smash and break it. Then there was the motor and fuel lines and the fuel tank, a steel container mounted on the center of gravity in front of the pilot, under the Vickers gun. Bullets could do horrible damage to fuel tanks and engines.

And there was the petrol in the fuel tank.

Of course the whole airplane was covered with dope, a highly flammable chemical that pulled the fabric drumhead tight. The smallest fire would ignite the whole plane, make it blaze like a torch.

A truck loomed on the road ahead, amid the running men. Dipping the nose a trifle, Hyde lined the thing up with the bead and ring sight and let fly with the machine guns. He put in a long burst, saw the flashes as the bullets struck the metal. He ceased fire and pulled up just enough to let his wheels miss the top of the truck.

Gray-clad figures were everywhere, lying on the ground and running and kneeling and shooting. He pushed the triggers and kicked the rudder back and forth to spray his bullets around.

He heard the Lewis stop and knew it must be out of shells. He waited until Cook raised his nose and followed him up in a loose formation. Only when well away from the ground did he pull the gun back on the Foster mount so that he could get at the drum. It came off easily enough. He put it in the storage bin and lifted another drum into place with both hands while he flew the plane with his knees.

Fumbling, straining to hold the heavy drum against the windblast, he got the thing seated, worked the bolt to chamber a round, then pushed the gun back up the rail until it locked. All this while he maneuvered the stick with his knees to stay in Cook's vicinity. Cook was similarly engaged changing his Lewis drum, so his plane was also flying erratically.

After the gun was reloaded Hyde looked around for Mac and Fitz-something. They were a mile or so to the left, under a gloomy cloud, descending onto another road.

He would stay with Nigel, who was going to fly back over the supply dump again! The blithering fool.

More fire from the ground, machine guns this time—

the muzzle flashes were unmistakable. If Cook wasn't careful the Germans were going to be shooting Big Bertha at him.

A hatful of bullets stitched Hyde's right wing, broke one of the bracing wires. Hyde wiggled the plane instinctively, then settled down to slaughter troops on the road ahead.

He opened fire. Walked the bullets into a mass of men and saw them fall, shot down a solitary grey figure in a coal-scuttle helmet who was shooting at him, toppled a team of horses pulling a wagon, gunned men lying in a ditch. . . .

A bullet burned the back of his hand, furrowed a gouge through the glove, and flesh and blood welled up.

Cook flew lower and lower, his guns going steadily. Hyde saw him out of the corner of his eye as he picked his own targets from the mass of men and horses and lorries on the road ahead.

His face felt hot. He ignored it for a few seconds, then paid attention. Hot. Droplets of a hot liquid.

The radiator was holed. He was losing water from the radiator.

And he was again out of ammo for the Lewis. He had another drum, so without waiting for Cook, he pulled up and soared away from the fray.

The Germans opened up with a flak gun. The bursts were so close the plane shook. He got the empty ammo drum off the gun, tossed it over the side. Got a fresh drum up and the gun ready.

As he turned to descend, he saw Cook's plane go into the ground. One second it was skimming the earth, the gun going nicely, then it was trailing a streak of flame. An eye-blink later the plane touched the earth and came apart in a welling smear of fire and smoke.

There were enemy troops everywhere he looked. Paul Hyde picked a concentration ahead and opened fire.

The hot water from the radiator was soaking him. There wasn't enough of it to scald him, just enough to get him wet.

Wiggling the rudder, holding the trigger down, Hyde shot at everything he saw. The Vickers ceased firing. Out of ammo, probably.

When the Lewis jammed he instinctively turned for the trenches. The water was hotter now, so it was coming out of the radiator in more volume. The needle on the water temp gauge on the panel was pegged right. The engine was going to seize in a moment.

And his feet were wet. Hyde looked down. Liquid running along the floorboards, toward the rear of the plane. A lot of liquid. His shoes and socks were soaked.

Water?

Sweet Jesus, it must be petrol. There must be bullet holes in the tank! He flew with his right hand while he worked the fuel pump with his left.

When he crossed the German trenches the motor started knocking. A cylinder wasn't firing—he could hear and feel the knocking. Backfires from the exhaust pipe. And some Hun was blasting away at him with a machine gun.

A violent vibration swept through the plane, then another.

The last enemy trench was behind. Ahead he could see the British trenches. At least this time he wasn't going to cross in the middle of an artillery barrage.

He crossed the trenches twenty feet in the air, the engine knocking loudly and vibrating as if it were going to jump off the mount.

He didn't have much speed left. He tried to hold the nose up and couldn't.

The wheels hit something and he bounced. Pulled the stick back into his lap and cut the switch. The noise stopped as the ship slowed and settled.

It bounced once more, then the landing gear assembly tore off and the fuselage slid along the mud and smacked over a shell hole and came, finally, to rest.

Paul Hyde was out and running before the plane stopped moving.

He was gone about seventy feet when fuel vapor found the hot metal parts of the engine and burst into flame. The *whuff* of the whole ship lighting off pushed Hyde forward on his face.

He lay there in the cold mud gripping the earth with both hands.

Finally he turned over in the slime and looked up at the evening sky.

Two Tommies found him there.

"Are you injured, sir?" they demanded, running their hands over him, feeling his body for wounds or broken bones.

He tried to answer and couldn't.

One of them held Hyde's head in his hands and looked straight into his eyes.

"It's all right, laddie," he said. "You're safe. You can stop screaming now."

Al-Jihad

ONE

Julie Giraud was crazy as hell. I knew that for an absolute fact, so I was contemplating what a real damned fool I was to get mixed up in her crazy scheme when I drove the Humvee and trailer into the belly of the V-22 Osprey and tied them down.

I quickly checked the stuff in the Humvee's trailer, made sure it was secure, then walked out of the Osprey and across the dark concrete ramp. Lights shining down from the peak of the hangar reflected in puddles of rainwater. The rain had stopped just at dusk, an hour or so ago.

I was the only human in sight amid the tiltrotor Ospreys parked on that vast mat. They looked like medium-sized transports except that they had an engine on each wingtip, and the engines were pointed straight up. Atop each engine was a thirty-eight-foot, three-bladed rotor. The engines were mounted on swivels that allowed them to be tilted from the vertical to the horizontal, giving the Ospreys the ability to take off and land like helicopters and then fly along in winged flight like the turboprop transports they really were.

I stopped by the door into the hangar and looked around again, just to make sure, then I opened the door and went inside.

The corridor was lit, but empty. My footsteps made a dull noise on the tile floor. I took the second right, into a ready room.

The duty officer was standing by the desk strapping a belt and holster to her waist. She was wearing a flight suit and black flying boots. Her dark hair was pulled back into a bun. She glanced at me. "Ready?"

"Where are all the security guards?"

"Watching a training film. They thought it was unusual to send everyone, but I insisted."

"I sure as hell hope they don't get suspicious."

She picked up her flight bag, took a last look around, and glanced at her watch. Then she grinned at me. "Let's go get 'em."

That was Julie Giraud, and as I have said, she was crazy as hell.

Me, I was just greedy. Three million dollars was a lot of kale, enough to keep me in beer and pretzels for the next hundred and ninety years. I followed this ding-a-ling bloodthirsty female along the hallway and through the puddles on the ramp to the waiting Osprey. Julie didn't run—she strode purposefully. If she was nervous or having second thoughts about committing the four dozen felonies we had planned for the next ten minutes, she sure didn't show it.

The worst thing I had ever done up to that point in my years on this planet was cheat a little on my income tax—no more than average, though—and here I was about to become a co-conspirator in enough crimes to keep a grand jury busy for a year. I felt like a condemned man on his way to the gallows, but the thought of all those smackers kept me marching along behind ol' crazy Julie.

We boarded the plane through the cargo door, and I closed it behind us.

Julie took three or four minutes to check our cargo, leaving nothing to chance. I watched her with grudging respect—crazy or not, she looked like a pro to me, and at my age I damn well didn't want to go tilting at windmills with an amateur.

When she finished her inspection, she led the way forward to the cockpit. She got into the left seat, her hands flew over the buttons and levers, arranging everything to her satisfaction. As I strapped myself into the right seat, she cranked the left engine. The RPMs came up nicely. The right engine was next.

As the radios warmed up, she quickly ran through the checklist, scanned gauges, and set up computer displays. I wasn't a pilot; everything I knew about the V-22 tiltrotor Osprey came from Julie, who wasn't given to longwinded explanations. If was almost as if every word she said cost her money.

While she did her pilot thing, I sat there looking out the windows, nervous as a cat on crack, trying to spot the platoon of FBI agents who were probably closing in to arrest us right that very minute. I didn't see anyone, of course: The parking mat of the air force base was as deserted as a nudist colony in January.

About that time Julie snapped on the aircraft's exterior lights, which made weird reflections on the other aircraft parked nearby, and the landing lights, powerful spotlights that shone on the concrete in front of us.

She called Ground Control on the radio. They gave her a clearance to a base in southern Germany, which she copied and read back flawlessly.

We weren't going to southern Germany, I knew, even if the air traffic controllers didn't. Julie released the brakes, and almost as if by magic, the Osprey began moving, taxiing along the concrete. She turned to pick up a taxiway, moving slowly, sedately, while she set up the computer displays on the instrument panel in front of her. There were two multifunction displays in front of me, too, and she leaned across to punch up the displays she wanted. I just watched. All this time we were rolling slowly along the endless taxiways lined with blue lights, across at least one runway, taxiing, taxiing . . . A rabbit ran across in front of us, through the beam of the taxi light.

Finally Julie stopped and spoke to the tower, which cleared us for takeoff.

"Are you ready?" she asked me curtly.

"For prison, hell, or what?"

She ignored that comment, which just slipped out. I was sitting there wondering how well I was going to adjust to institutional life.

She taxied onto the runway, lined up the plane, then advanced the power lever with her left hand. I could hear the engines winding up, feel the power of the giant rotors tearing at the air, trying to lift this twenty-eight-ton beast from the earth's grasp.

The Osprey rolled forward on the runway, slowly at first, and when it was going a little faster than a man could run, lifted majestically into the air.

The crime was consummated.

We had just stolen a forty-million-dollar V-22 Osprey, snatched it right out of Uncle Sugar's rather loose grasp, not to mention a half million dollars' worth of other miscellaneous military equipment that was carefully stowed in the back of the plane.

Now for the getaway.

In seconds Julie began tilting the engines down to transition to forward flight. The concrete runway slid under us, faster and faster as the Osprey accelerated. She snapped up the wheels, used the stick to raise the nose of the plane. The airspeed indicator read over 140 knots as the end of the runway disappeared into the darkness below and the night swallowed us.

Two weeks before that evening, Julie Giraud drove into my filling station in Van Nuys. I didn't know her then, of course. I was sitting in the office reading the morning paper. I glanced out, saw her pull up to the pump in a new white sedan. She got out of the car and used a credit card at the pump, so I went back to the paper.

I had only owned that gasoline station for about a week, but I had already figured out why the previous owner sold it so cheap: The mechanic was a doper and the guy running the register was a thief. I was contemplating various ways of solving those two problems when the woman with the white sedan finished pumping her gas and came walking toward the office.

She was a bit over medium height, maybe thirty years old, a hard-body wearing a nice outfit that must have set her back a few bills. She looked vaguely familiar, but this close to Hollywood, you often see people you think you ought to know.

She came straight over to where I had the little chair tilted back against the wall and asked, "Charlie Dean?"

"Yeah."

"I'm Julie Giraud. Do you remember me?"

It took me a few seconds. I put the paper down and got up from the chair.

"It's been a lot of years," I said.

"Fifteen, I think. I was just a teenager."

"Colonel Giraud's eldest daughter. I remember. Do you have a sister a year or two younger?"

"Rachael. She's a dental tech, married with two kids."

"I sorta lost track of your father, I guess. How is he?"

"Dead."

"Well, I'm sorry."

I couldn't think of anything else to say. Her dad had

been my commanding officer at the antiterrorism school, but that was years ago. I went on to other assignments, and finally retired five years ago with thirty years in. I hadn't seen or thought of the Girauds in years.

"I remember Dad remarking several times that you were the best Marine in the corps."

That comment got the attention of the guy behind the register. His name was Candy. He had a few tattoos on his arms and a half dozen rings dangling from various portions of his facial anatomy. He looked at me now with renewed interest.

I tried to concentrate on Julie Giraud. She was actually a good-looking woman, with her father's square chin and good cheekbones. She wasn't wearing makeup: She didn't need any.

"I remember him telling us that you were a sniper in Vietnam, and the best Marine in the corps."

Candy's eyebrows went up toward his hairline when he heard that.

"I'm flattered that you remember me, Ms. Giraud, but I'm a small-business owner now. I left the Marines five years ago." I gestured widely. "This grand establishment belongs to me and the hundreds of thousands of stockholders in the Bank of America. All of us thank you for stopping by today and giving us your business."

She nodded, turned toward the door, then hesitated. "I wonder if we might have lunch together, Mr. Dean."

Why not? "Okay. Across the street at the Burger King, in about an hour?" That was agreeable with her. She got in her car and drove away.

Amazing how people from the past pop back into your life when you least expect it.

I tilted the chair back, lifted my paper, and sat there wondering what in hell Julie Giraud could possibly want to talk about with me. Candy went back to his copy of *Rolling Stone*. In a few minutes two people came in and paid cash for their gas. With the paper hiding my face, I could look into a mirror I had mounted on the ceiling and watch Candy handle the money. I put the mirror up there three days ago, but if he noticed, he had forgotten it by now.

As the second customer left, Candy pocketed something. I didn't know if he shortchanged the customer or just helped himself to a bill from the till. The tally and the tape hadn't been jibing and Candy had a what-are-you-gonna-do-about-it-old-man attitude.

He closed the till and glanced at me with a look that could only be amusement.

I folded the paper, put it down, got out of the chair, and went over to the counter.

"So you was in the Marines, huh?"

"Yeah."

He grinned confidently. "Wouldn't have figured that."

I reached, grabbed a ring dangling from his eyebrow, and ripped it out.

Candy screamed. Blood flowed from the eyebrow. He recoiled against the register with a look of horror on his face.

"The money, kid. Put it on the counter."

He glanced at the blood on his hand, then pressed his hand against his eyebrow trying to stanch the flow. "You bastard! I don't know what you—"

Reaching across the counter, I got a handful of hair with my left hand and the ring in his nose with my right. "You want to lose all these, one by one?"

He dug in his pocket, pulled out a wadded bill and threw it on the counter.

"You're fired, kid. Get off the property and never come back."

He came around the counter, trying to stay away from me, one hand on his bleeding eyebrow. He stopped in the door. "I'll get you for this, you son of a bitch."

"You think that through, kid. Better men than you have died trying. If you just gotta do it, though, you know where to find me."

He scurried over to his twenty-five-year-old junker Pontiac. He ground and ground with the starter. Just when I thought he would have to give up, the motor belched a cloud of blue smoke.

I got on the phone to a friend of mine, also a retired Marine. His name was Bill Wiley, and he worked full time as a police dispatcher. He agreed to come over that evening to help me out for a few hours at the station.

It seemed to me that I might as well solve all my problems in one day, so I went into the garage to see the mechanic, a long-haired Mexican named Juan.

"I think you've got an expensive habit, Juan. To pay for it you've been charging customers for work you didn't do, new parts you didn't install, then splitting the money with Candy. He hit the road. You can work honest from now on or leave, your choice."

"You can't prove shit."

He was that kind of guy, stupid as dirt. "I don't have to prove anything," I told him. "You're fired."

He didn't argue; he just went. I finished fixing the flat he had been working on, waited on customers until noon, then locked the place up and walked across the street to the Burger King.

Of course I was curious. It seemed doubtful that Julie Giraud wanted to spend an hour of her life reminiscing about the good old days at Quantico with a retired enlisted man who once served under her father, certainly not one twenty-five years older than she was.

So what did she want?

"You are not an easy man to find, Mr. Dean."

I shrugged. I'm not trying to lose myself in the madding crowd, but I'm not advertising either.

"My parents died twelve years ago," she said, her eyes on my face.

"Both of them?" I hadn't heard. "Sorry to hear that," I said.

"They were on an Air France flight to Paris that blew up over Niger. A bomb."

"Twelve years ago."

"Dad had been retired for just a year. He and Mom

were traveling, seeing the world, falling in love with each other all over again. They were on their way to Paris from South America when the plane blew up, killing every-one aboard."

I lost my appetite for hamburger. I put it down and sipped some coffee.

She continued, telling me her life story. She spent a few more years in high school, went to the Air Force Academy, was stationed in Europe flying V-22 Ospreys, was back in the States just now on leave.

When she wound down, I asked, as gently as I could, why she looked me up.

She opened her purse, took out a newspaper clipping, offered it to me. "Last year a French court tried the men who killed my parents. They are Libyans. Moammar Gadhafi refused to extradite them from Libya, so the French tried them in absentia, convicted them, sentenced them to life in prison."

I remembered reading about the trial. The clipping merely refreshed my memory. One hundred forty people died when that Air France flight exploded; the debris was scattered over fifty square miles of desert.

"Six men, and they are still in Libya." Julie gestured at the newspaper clipping, which was lying beside my food tray. "One of the men is Gadhafi's brother-in-law, another is a key figure in Libyan intelligence, two are in the Libyan diplomatic service." She gripped the little table between us and leaned forward. "They blew up that airliner on Gadhafi's order to express the dictator's displeasure with French foreign policy at the time. It was raw political terrorism, Mr. Dean, by a nation without the guts or wit to wage war. They just murder civilians."

I folded the clipping, then handed it back.

"Ms. Giraud, I'm sorry that your parents are dead. I'm sorry about all those people who died on that airliner. I'm sorry the men who murdered them are beyond the reach of the law. I'm sorry the French government hasn't got the guts or wit to clean out the vermin in Tripoli. But what has this got to do with me?"

"I want you to help me kill those men," she whispered, her voice as hard as a bayonet blade.

TWO

I grew up in a little town in southwestern Missouri. Dad was a welder and Mom waited tables in a diner, and both of them had trouble with the bottle. The afternoon of the day I graduated from high school I joined the Marines to get the hell out.

Sure, I killed my share of gomers in Vietnam. By then I thought life was a fairly good idea and wanted more of it. If I had to zap gomers to keep getting older, that was all right by me. It helped that I had a natural talent with a rifle. I was a medium-smart, whang-leather kid who never complained and did what I was told, so I eventually ended up in Force Recon. It took me a while to fit in; once I did, I was in no hurry to leave. Recon was the place where the Marine Corps kept its really tough men. The way I figured it, those guys were my life insurance.

That's the way it worked out. The guys in Recon kept each other alive. And we killed gomers.

All that was long ago and far away from Julie Giraud. She was the daughter of a Marine colonel, sure, a grad of the Air Force Academy, and she looked like she ran five miles or so every day, but none of that made her tough. Sitting across the table looking at her, I couldn't figure out if she was a fighter or a get-even, courthouse-stairs back-shooter. A lot of people like the abstract idea of revenge, of getting even, but they aren't willing to suffer much for the privilege. Sitting in Burger King watching Julie Giraud, listening to her tell me how she wanted to kill the men who had killed her parents, I tried to decide just how much steel was in her backbone.

Her dad had been a career officer with his share of Vietnam chest cabbage. When they were young a lot of the gung ho officers thought they were bulletproof and let it all hang out. When they eventually realized they were as mortal as everyone else and started sending sergeants to lead the patrols, they already had enough medals to decorate a Panamanian dictator. Whether Julie Giraud's dad was like that, I never knew.

A really tough man knows he is mortal, knows the dangers involved to the tenth decimal place, and goes ahead anyway. He is careful, committed, and absolutely ruthless.

After she dropped the bomb at lunch, I thought about these things for a while. Up to that point I had no idea why she had gone to the trouble of looking me up; the thought that she might want my help getting even with somebody never once zipped across the synapses. I took my time thinking things over before I said, "What's the rest of it?"

"It's a little complicated."

"Maybe you'd better lay it out."

"Outside, in my car."

"No. Outside on the sidewalk."

We threw the remnants of our lunch in the trash and went outside.

Julie Giraud looked me in the eye and explained, "These men are instruments of the Libyan government—"

"I got that point earlier."

"—seventeen days from now, on the twenty-third of this month, they are going to meet with members of three Middle East terrorist organizations and a representative of Saddam Hussein's government. They hope to develop a joint plan that Saddam will finance to attack targets throughout western Europe and the Middle East."

"Did you get a press release on this or what?"

"I have a friend, a fellow Air Force Academy graduate, who is now with the CIA."

"He just casually tells you this stuff?"

"She. She told me about the conference. And there is nothing casual about it. She knows what these people have cost me."

"Say you win the lottery and off a few of these guys, what's she gonna tell the internal investigators when they come around?"

Julie Giraud shook her head. "We're covered, believe me."

"I don't, but you're the one trying to make a sale, not me."

She nodded, then continued: "Seventeen days from now the delegates to this little conference will fly to an airstrip near an old fortress in the Sahara. The fortress is near an oasis on an old caravan route in the middle of nowhere. Originally built by the ancient Egyptians, the fortress was used by Carthaginians and Romans to guard that caravan route. The Foreign Legion did extensive restoration and kept a small garrison there for years. During World War II the Germans and British even had a little firefight there."

I grunted. She was intense, committed. Fanatics scare me, and she was giving me those vibes now.

"The fortress is on top of a rock ridge," she explained. "The Arabs call it the Camel."

"Never heard of it," I retorted. Of course there was no reason that I should have heard of the place—I was grasping at straws. I didn't like anything about this tale.

She was holding her purse loosely by the strap, so I grabbed it out of her hand. Her eyes narrowed; she thought about slapping me—actually shifted her weight to do it—then decided against it.

There was a small, round, poured-concrete picnic table there beside the Burger King for mothers to sit at while watching their kids play on the gym equipment, so I sat down and dug her wallet out of the purse. It contained a couple hundred in bills, a Colorado driver's license—she was twenty-eight years old—a military ID, three bank credit cards, an expired AAA membership, car insurance from USAA, a Sears credit card, and an ATM card in a paper envelope with her secret PIN number written on the envelope in ink.

Also in the wallet was a small, bound address book containing handwritten names, addresses, telephone numbers, and e-mail addresses. I flipped through the book, studying the names, then returned it to the wallet.

Her purse contained the usual feminine hygiene and cosmetic items. At the bottom were four old dry cleaning receipts from the laundry on the German base where she was stationed and a small collection of loose keys. One safety pin, two buttons, a tiny rusty screwdriver, a pair of sunglasses with a cracked lens, five European coins, and two U.S. quarters. One of the receipts was eight months old.

I put all this stuff back in her purse and passed it across the table.

"Okay," I said. "For the sake of argument, let's assume you're telling the truth—that there really is a terrorists' conference scheduled at an old pile of Foreign Legion masonry in the middle of the goddamn Sahara seventeen days from now. What do you propose to do about it?"

"I propose to steal a V-22 Osprey," Julie Giraud said evenly, "fly there, plant enough C-4 to blow that old fort to kingdom come, then wait for the terrorists to arrive. When they are all sitting in there plotting who they are going to murder next, I'm going to push the button and send the whole lot of them straight to hell. Just like they did to my parents and everyone else on that French DC-10."

"You and who else?"

The breeze was playing with her hair. "You and me," she said. "The two of us."

I tried to keep a straight face. Across the street at my filling station people were standing beside their cars, waiting impatiently for me to get back and open up. That was paying business and I was sitting here listening to this shit. The thought that the CIA or FBI might be recording this conversation also crossed my mind.

"You're a nice kid, Julie. Thanks for dropping by. I'm sorry about your folks, but there is nothing on earth anyone can do for them. It's time to lay them to rest. Fly high, meet a nice guy, fall in love, have some kids, give them the best that you have in you: Your parents would have wanted that for you. The fact is they're gone and you can't bring them back."

She brushed the hair back from her eyes. "If you'll help me, Mr. Dean, I'll pay you three million dollars."

I didn't know what to say. Three million dollars rated serious consideration, but I couldn't tell if she had what it takes to make it work.

"I'll think about it," I said, and got up. "Tomorrow, we'll have lunch again right here."

She showed some class then. "Okay," she said, and nodded once. She didn't argue or try to make the sale right then, and I appreciated that.

. . .

My buddy, Gunnery Sergeant Bill Wiley, left the filling station at ten that night; I had to stay until closing time at 2 A.M. About midnight an older four-door Chrysler cruised slowly past on the street, for the second or third time, and I realized the people inside were casing the joint.

Ten minutes later, when the pumps were vacant and I was the only person in the store, the Chrysler drove in fast and stopped in front of the door. My ex–cash register man, Candy, boiled out of the passenger seat with a gun in his hand, a 9-mm automatic. He and the guy from the backseat came charging through the door waving their guns at me.

"Hands up, Charlie Dean, you silly son of a bitch. We want all the money, and if you ain't real goddamn careful I'm gonna blow your fucking brains out."

The guy from the backseat posted himself by the door and kept glancing up and down the street to see who was driving by. The driver of the car stayed outside.

Candy strutted over to me and stuck his gun in my face. He had a butterfly bandage on his eyebrow. He was about to say something really nasty, I think, when I grabbed his gun with my left hand and hit him with all I had square in the mouth with my right. He went down like he had been sledgehammered. I leaped toward the other one and hit him in the head with the gun butt, and he went down, too. Squatting, I grabbed his gun while I checked the driver outside.

The driver was standing frozen beside the car, staring through the plate-glass window at me like I was Godzilla. I already had the safety off on Candy's automatic, so I swung it into the middle of this dude's chest and pulled the trigger.

Click.

Oh boy!

As I got the other pistol up, the third man dived behind the wheel and slammed the Chrysler into gear. That pistol also clicked uselessly. The Chrysler left in a squall of rubber and exhaust smoke.

I checked the pistols one at a time. Both empty.

Candy's eyes were trying to focus, so I bent down and asked him, "How come you desperate characters came in here with empty pistols?"

He spit blood and a couple teeth as he thought about it. His lips were swelling. He was going to look like holy hell for a few days. Finally one eye focused. "Didn't want to shoot you," he mumbled, barely understandable. "Just scare you."

"Umm."

"The guns belong to my dad. He didn't have any bullets around."

"Did the driver of the car know the guns were empty?"

Candy nodded, spit some more blood.

I'll admit, I felt kind of sorry for Candy. He screwed up the courage to go after a pint or two of revenge, but the best he could do for backup help was a coward who ran from empty pistols.

I put the guns in the trash can under the register and

got each of them a bottled water from the cooler. They were slowly coming around when a police cruiser with lights flashing pulled up between the pumps and the office and the officer jumped out. He came striding in with his hand on the butt of his pistol.

"Someone called in on their cell phone, reported a robbery in progress here."

I kept my hands in plain sight where he could see them. "No robbery, officer. My name's Dean; I own this filling station."

"What happened to these two?" Spittle and blood were smeared on one front of Candy's shirt, and his friend had a dilly of a shiner.

"They had a little argument," I explained, "slugged each other. This fellow here, Candy, works for me."

Candy and his friend looked at me kind of funny, but they went along with it. After writing down everyone's names and addresses from their driver's licenses while I expanded on my fairy tale, the officer left.

Candy and his friend were on their feet by then. "I'm sorry, Mr. Dean," Candy said.

"Tell you what, kid. You want to play it straight, no stealing and no shortchanging people, you come back to work in the morning."

"You mean that?"

"Yeah." I dug his father's guns from the trash and handed them to him. "You better take these home and put them back where they belong."

His face was red and he was having trouble talking. "I'll be here," he managed.

He pocketed the pistols, nodded, then he and his friend went across the street to Burger King to call someone to come get them.

I was shaking so bad I had to sit down. Talk about luck! If the pistols had been loaded I would have killed that fool kid driving the car, and I didn't even know if he had a gun. That could have cost me life in the pen. Over what?

I sat there in the office thinking about life and death and Julie Giraud.

At lunch the next day Julie Giraud was intense, yet cool as she talked of killing people, slaughtering them like steers. I'd seen my share of people with that look. She was just flat crazy.

The fact that she was a nut seemed to explain a lot, somehow. If she had been sane I would have turned her down flat. It's been my experience through the years that sane people who go traipsing off to kill other people usually get killed themselves. The people who do best at combat don't have a death grip on life, if you know what I mean. They are crazy enough to take the biggest risk of all and not freak out when the shooting starts. Julie Giraud looked like she had her share of that kind of insanity.

"Do I have my information correct? Were you a sniper in Vietnam, Mr. Dean?"

"That was a war," I said, trying to find the words to explain, taking my time. "I was in Recon. We did ambushes and assassinations. I had a talent with a rifle.

Other men had other talents. What you're suggesting isn't war, Ms. Giraud."

"Do you still have what it takes?"

She was goading me and we both knew it. I shrugged.

She wouldn't let it alone. "Could you still kill a man at five hundred yards with a rifle? Shoot him down in cold blood?"

"You want me to shoot somebody today so you can see if I'm qualified for the job?"

"I'm willing to pay three million dollars, Mr. Dean, to the man with the balls to help me kill the men who murdered my parents. I'm offering you the job. I'll pay half up front into a Swiss bank account, half after we kill the men who killed my parents."

"What if you don't make it? What if they kill you?"

"I'll leave a wire transfer order with my banker."

I snorted. At times I got the impression she thought this was some kind of extreme sports expedition, like jumping from a helicopter to ski down a mountain. And yet . . . she had that fire in her eyes.

"Where in hell did a captain in the air farce get three million dollars?"

"I inherited half my parents' estate and invested it in software and Internet stocks; and the stocks went up like a rocket shot to Mars, as everyone north of Antarctica well knows. Now I'm going to spend the money on something I want very badly. That's the American way, isn't it?"

"Like ribbed condoms and apple pie," I agreed, then leaned forward to look into her eyes. "If we kill these men," I explained, "the world will never be the same for you. When you look in the mirror the face that stares back won't be the same one you've been looking at all these years—it'll be uglier. Your parents will still be dead and you'll be older in ways that years can't measure. That's the god's truth, kid. Your parents are going to be dead regardless. Keep your money, find a good guy, and have a nice life."

She sneered. "You're a philosopher?"

"I've been there, lady. I'm trying to figure out if I want to go back."

"Three million dollars, Mr. Dean. How long will it take for your gasoline station to make three million dollars profit?"

I owned three gas stations, all mortgaged to the hilt, but I wasn't going to tell her that. I sat in the corner of Burger King working on a Diet Coke while I thought about the kid I had damn near killed the night before.

"What about afterward?" I asked. "Tell me how you and I are going to continue to reside on this planet with the CIA and FBI and Middle Eastern terrorists all looking to carve on our ass."

She knew a man, she said, who could provide passports.

"Fake passports? Bullshit! Get real."

"Genuine passports. He's a U.S. consular official in Munich."

"What are you paying him?"

"He wants to help."

"Dying to go to prison, is he?"

"I've slept with him for the past eighteen months."

"You got a nice ass, but . . . Unless this guy is a real toad, he can get laid any night of the week. Women today think if they don't use it, they'll wear it out pissing through it."

"You have difficulty expressing yourself in polite company, don't you, Charlie Dean? Okay, cards on the table: I'm fucking him and paying him a million dollars."

I sat there thinking it over.

"If you have the money you can buy anything," she said.

"I hope you aren't foolish enough to believe that."

"Someone always wants money. All you have to do is find that someone. You're a case in point."

"How much would it cost to kill an ex-Marine who became a liability and nuisance?"

"A lot less than I'm paying you," she shot back. She didn't smile.

After a bit she started talking again, telling me how we were going to kill the bad guys. I didn't think much of her plan—blow up a stone fortress?—but I sat there listening while I mulled things over. Three million was not small change.

Finally I decided that Julie's conscience was her problem and the three million would look pretty good in my bank account. The Libyans—well, I really didn't give a damn about them one way or the other. They would squash me like a bug if they thought I was any threat at all, so what the hell. They had blown up airliners, they could take their chances with the devil.

THREE

We were inside a rain cloud. Water ran off the windscreen in continuous streams: The dim glow of the red cockpit lights made the streams look like pale red rivers. Beyond the wet windscreen, however, the night was coal black.

I had never seen such absolute darkness.

Julie Giraud had the Osprey on autopilot; she was bent over fiddling with the terrain-avoidance radar while auto flew the plane.

I sure as hell wasn't going to be much help. I sat there watching her, wondering if I had made a sucker's deal. Three million was a lot of money if you lived to spend it. If you died earning it, it was nowhere near enough.

After a bit she turned off the radios and some other

electronic gear, then used the autopilot to drop the nose into a descent. The multifunction displays in front of us—there were four plus a radar screen—displayed engine data, our flight plan, a moving map, and one that appeared to be a tactical display of the locations of the radars that were looking at us. I certainly didn't understand much of it, and Julie Giraud was as loquacious as a store dummy.

"We'll drop off their radar screens now," she muttered finally in way of explanation. As if to emphasize our departure into the outlaw world, she snapped off the plane's exterior lights.

As the altimeter unwound I must have looked a little nervous, and I guess I was. I rode two helicopters into the ground in Vietnam and one in Afghanistan, all shot down, so in the years since I had tried to avoid anything with rotors. Jets didn't bother me much, but rotor whop made my skin crawl.

Down we went until we were flying through the valleys of the Bavarian Alps below the hilltops. Julie sat there twiddling the autopilot as we flew along, keeping us between the hills with the radar.

She looked cool as a tall beer in July. "How come you aren't a little nervous?" I asked.

"This is the easy part," she replied.

That shut me up.

We were doing about 270 knots, so it took a little while to thread our way across Switzerland and northern Italy to the ocean. Somewhere over Italy we flew out of the rain. I breathed a sigh of relief when we left the valleys behind and dropped to a hundred feet over the ocean. Julie turned the plane for Africa.

"How do you know fighters aren't looking for us in this goop?" I asked.

She pointed toward one of the multifunction displays. "That's a threat indicator. We'll see anyone who uses a radar."

After a while I got bored, even at a hundred feet, so I got unstrapped and went aft to check the Humvee, trailer, and cargo.

All secure.

I opened my duffel bag, got out a pistol belt. The gun, an old 1911 Colt .45 automatic, was loaded, but I checked it anyway, reholstered it, got the belt arranged around my middle so it rode comfortable with the pistol on my right side and my Ka-Bar knife on the left. I also had another knife in one boot and a hideout pistol in the other, just in case.

I put a magazine in the M-16 but didn't chamber a round. I had disassembled the weapon the night before, cleaned it thoroughly, and oiled it lightly.

The last weapon in the bag was a Model 70 in .308. It was my personal rifle, one I had built up myself years ago. With a synthetic stock, a Canjar adjustable trigger, and a heavy barrel custom-made for me by a Colorado gunsmith, it would put five shots into a half-inch circle at a hundred yards with factory match-grade ammunition. I had the 3×9 adjustable scope zeroed for two hundred. Trigger pull was exactly eighteen ounces.

I repacked the rifles, then sat in the driver's seat of

the Humvee and poured myself a cup of coffee from the thermos.

We flew to Europe on different airlines and arrived in Zurich just hours apart. The following day I opened a bank account at a gleaming pile of marble in the heart of the financial district. As I watched, Julie called her banker in Virginia and had $1.5 million in cold hard cash transferred into the account. Three hours after she made the transfer I went to my bank and checked: The money was really there and it was all mine.

Amazing.

We met for dinner at a little hole-in-the-wall restaurant a few blocks off the main drag that I remembered from years before, when I was sight-seeing while on leave during a tour in Germany.

"The money's there," I told her when we were seated. "I confess, I didn't think it would be."

She got a little huffy. "I'd lie to you?"

"It's been known to happen. Though for the life of me, I couldn't see why you would."

She opened her purse, handed me an unsealed envelope. Inside was a passport. I got up and went to the men's room, where I inspected it. It certainly looked like a genuine U.S. passport, on the right paper and printed with dots and displaying my shaved, honest phiz. The name on the thing was Robert Arnold. I put it in my jacket pocket and rejoined her at the table.

She handed me a letter and an addressed envelope.

The letter was to her banker, typed, instructing him to transfer another $1.5 million to my account a week after we were scheduled to hit the Camel. The envelope was addressed to him and even had a Swiss stamp on it. I checked the numbers on my account at the Swiss bank. Everything jibed.

She had a pen in her hand by that time. After she had signed the letter, I sealed it in the envelope, then folded the envelope and tucked it in my pocket beside the passport.

"Okay, lady. I'm bought and paid for."

We made our plans over dinner. She drank one glass of wine, and I had a beer, then we both switched to mineral water. I told her I wanted my own pistol and rifles, a request she didn't blink at. She agreed to fly into Dover Air Force Base on one of the regularly scheduled cargo runs, then take my duffel bag containing the weapons back to Germany with her.

"What if someone wants to run the bag through a metal detector, or German customs wants to inspect it?"

"My risk."

"I guess there are a few advantages to being a well-scrubbed, clean-cut American girl."

"You can get away with a lot if you shave your legs."

"I'll keep that in mind."

That was ten days ago. Now we were on our way. Tomorrow we were going to case the old fort and come up with a plan for doing in the assembled bad guys.

Sitting in the driver's seat of the Humvee sipping coffee and listening to the drone of the turboprops carrying us across the Mediterranean, I got the old combat feeling again.

Yeah, this was really it.

Only this time I was going to get paid for it.

I finished the coffee, went back to the cockpit, and offered Julie a cup. She was intent on the computer screens.

"Problems?" I asked.

"I'm picking up early warning radar, but I think I'm too low for the Libyans to see me. There's a fighter aloft, too. I doubt if he can pick us out of ground return."

All that was outside my field of expertise. On this portion of the trip, I was merely a passenger.

I saw the land appear on the radar presentation, watched it march down the scope toward us, as if we were stationary and the world was turning under us. It was a nice illusion. As we crossed the beach, I checked my watch. We were only a minute off our planned arrival time, which seemed to me to be a tribute to Julie's piloting skills.

The ride got bumpy over the desert. Even at night the thermals kept the air boiling. Julie Giraud took the plane off autopilot, hand-flew it. Trusting the autopilot in rough air so close to the ground was foolhardy.

I got out the chart, used a little red spotlight mounted on the ceiling of the cockpit to study the lines and notes as we bounced along in turbulence.

We had an hour and twenty minutes to go. Fuel to

get out of the desert would have been a problem, so we had brought five hundred gallons in a portable tank in the cargo compartment. Tomorrow night we would use a hand pump to transfer that fuel into the plane's tanks, enough to get us out of Africa when the time came.

I sat back and watched her fly, trying not to think about the tasks and dangers ahead. At some point it doesn't pay to worry about hazards you can't do anything about. When you've taken all the precautions you can, then it's time to think about something else.

The landing site we had picked was seven miles from the Camel, at the base of what appeared on the chart to be a cliff. The elevation lines seemed to indicate a cliff of sixty or seventy feet in height.

"How do you know that is a cliff?" I had asked Julie when she first showed the chart to me. In reply she pulled out two satellite photos. They had obviously been taken at different times of day, perhaps in different seasons or years, but they were obviously of the same piece of terrain. I compared them to the chart.

There was a cliff all right, and apparently room to tuck the Osprey in against it, pretty much out of sight.

"You want me to try to guess where you got these satellite photos?"

"My friend in the CIA."

"And nobody is going to ask her any questions?"

"Nope. She's cool and she's clean."

"I don't buy it."

"She doesn't have access to this stuff. She's stealing it. They'll only talk to people with access."

"Must be a bunch of stupes in the IG's office there, huh."

She wouldn't say any more.

We destroyed the photos, of course, before we left the apartment she had rented for me. Still, the thought of Julie's classmate in the CIA who could sell us down the river to save her own hide gave me a sick feeling in the pit of my stomach as we motored through the darkness over the desert.

Julie had our destination dialed into the navigation computer, so the magic box was depicting our track and time to go. I sat there watching the miles and minutes tick down.

With five miles to go, Julie began slowing the Osprey. And she flipped on the landing lights. Beams of light seared the darkness and revealed the yellow rock and sand and dirt of the deep desert.

She began tilting the engines toward the vertical, which slowed us further and allowed the giant rotors to begin carrying a portion of our weight.

When the last mile ticked off the computer and we crossed the cliff line, the Osprey was down to fifty knots. Julie brought the V-22 into a hover and used the landing lights to explore our hiding place. Some small boulders, not too many, and the terrain under the cliff was relatively flat.

After a careful circuit and inspection, Julie set the Osprey down, shut down the engines.

The silence was startling as we took off our helmets.

Now she shut down the aircraft battery and all the cockpit lights went off.

"We're here," she said with a sigh of relief.

"You really intend to go through with this, don't you?"

"Don't tell me you still have doubts, Charlie Dean."

"Okay. I won't."

She snapped on a flashlight and led the way back through the cargo bay. She opened the rear door and we stepped out onto the godforsaken soil of the Sahara. We used a flashlight to inspect our position.

"I could get it a little closer to the cliff, but I doubt if it's worth the effort."

"Let's get to work," I said. I was tired of sitting.

First she went back to the cockpit and tilted the engines down to the cruise position. The plane would be easier to camouflage with the engines down. We would rotate the engines back to the vertical position when the time came to leave.

Next we unloaded the Humvee and trailer, then the cargo we had tied down in piles on the floor of the plane. I carried the water jugs out myself, taking care to place them where they wouldn't fall over.

The last thing we removed from the plane was the camouflage netting. We unrolled it, then began draping it over the airplane. We both had to get up on top of the plane to get the net over the tail and engine nacelles. Obviously we couldn't cover the blade of each rotor that stuck straight up, so we cut holes in the net for them.

It took us almost two hours of intense effort to get

the net completely rigged. We treated ourselves to a drink of water.

"We sure can't get out of here in a hurry," I remarked.

"I swore on the altar of God I would kill the men who killed my parents. We aren't going anywhere until we do it."

"Yeah."

I finished my drink, then unhooked the trailer from the Humvee and dug out my night-vision goggles. I uncased my Model 70 and chambered a round, put on the safety, then got into the driver's seat and laid it across my lap.

"We can't plant explosives until tomorrow night," she said.

"I know that. But I want a look at that place now. You coming?"

She got her night-vision goggles and climbed into the passenger seat. I took the time to fire up the GPS and key in our destination, then started the Humvee and plugged in my night-vision goggles. It was like someone turned on the light. I could see the cliff and the plane and the stones as if the sun were shining on an overcast day.

I put the Humvee in gear and rolled.

FOUR

The Camel sat on a granite ridge that humped up out of the desert floor. On the eastern side of the ridge, in the low place scooped out by the wind, there was an oasis, a small pond of muddy water, a few palm trees, and a cluster of mud huts. According to Julie's CIA sister, a few dozen nomads lived here seasonally. Standing on the hood of the Humvee, which was parked on a gentle rise a mile east of the oasis, I could just see the tops of the palms and a few of the huts. No heat source flared up when I switched to infrared.

The old fort was a shattered hulk upon the skyline, brooding and massive. The structure itself wasn't large, but perched there on that granite promontory it was a presence.

I slowly did a 360-degree turn, sweeping the desert.

Nothing moved. I saw only rock and hard-packed earth, here and there a scraggly desert plant. The wind had long ago swept away the sand.

Finally I got down off the hood of the Humvee. Julie was standing there with her arms crossed looking cold, although the temperature was at least sixty.

"I want you to drive this thing back into that draw, and just sit and wait. I'm going to walk over there and eyeball it up."

"When are you coming back?"

"Couple hours after dawn, probably. I want to make sure there are no people there, and I want to see it in the daylight."

"Can't we just wait until tonight to check it out?"

"I'm not going to spend a day not knowing what in hell is over the hill. I didn't get to be this old by taking foolish risks. Drive down there and wait for me."

She got in the Humvee and did as I asked.

I adjusted my night-vision goggles, tucked the Model 70 under my arm, and started hiking.

I had decided on South Africa. After this was over, I was going to try South Africa. I figured it would be middling difficult for the Arabs to root me out there. I had never been to South Africa, but from everything I had seen and heard the country sounded like it might have a future now that they had made a start at solving the racial problem. South Africa. My image of the place had a bit of a Wild West flavor that appealed to my sporting instincts.

Not that I really have any sporting instincts. Those all got squeezed out of me in Vietnam. I'd rather shoot the bastards in the back than in the front: It's safer.

The CIA and FBI? They could find me anywhere, if they wanted to. The theft of a V-22 wasn't likely to escape their notice, but I didn't think the violent death of some terrorists would inspire those folks to put in a lot of overtime. I figured a fellow who stayed out of sight would soon be out of mind, too.

With three million dollars in my jeans, staying out of sight would be a pleasure.

That's the way I had it figured, anyhow. As I walked across the desert hardpan toward the huts by the mudhole, I confess, I was thinking again about South Africa, which made me angry.

Concentrate, I told myself. Stay focused. Stay alive.

I was glad the desert here was free of sand. I was leaving no tracks in the hard-packed earth and stone of the desert floor that I could see or feel with my fingers, which relieved me somewhat.

I took my time approaching the huts from downwind. No dogs that I could see, no vehicles, no sign of people. The place looked deserted.

And was. Not a soul around. I checked all five of the huts, looked in the sheds. Not even a goat or puppy.

There were marks of livestock by the water hole. Only

six inches of water, I estimated, at the deepest part. At the widest place the pond was perhaps thirty feet across, about the size of an Iowa farm pond but with less water.

The cliff loomed above the back of the water hole. Sure enough, I found a trail. I started climbing.

The top of the ridge was about three hundred feet above the surrounding terrain. I huffed and puffed a bit getting up there. On top there was a little breeze blowing, a warm, dry desert breeze that felt delicious at that hour of the night.

I found a vantage point and examined the fort through the night-vision goggles, looked all around in every direction. To the west I could see the paved strip of the airport reflecting the starlight, so it appeared faintly luminescent. It too was empty. No people, no planes, no vehicles, no movement, just stone and great empty places.

I took off the goggles and turned them off to save the battery, then waited for my eyes to adjust to the darkness. The stars were so close in that clear dry air it seemed as if I could reach up and touch them. To the east the sky was lightening up.

As the dawn slowly chased away the night, I worked my way toward the fort, which was about a third of a mile from where the trail topped the ridge. Fortunately there were head-high clumps of desert brush tucked into the nooks and crannies of the granite, so I tried to stay under cover as much as possible. By the time the sun poked its head over the earth's rim I was standing under the wall of the fort.

I listened.

All I could hear was the whisper of the wind.

I found a road and a gate, which wasn't locked. After all, how many people are running around out here in this wasteland?

Taking my time, I sneaked in. I had the rifle off my shoulder and leveled, with my thumb on the safety and my finger on the trigger.

A Land Rover was parked in the courtyard. It had a couple five-gallon cans strapped to the back of it and was caked with dirt and dust. The tires were relatively new, sporting plenty of tread.

When I was satisfied no one was in the courtyard, I stepped over to the Land Rover. The keys were in the ignition.

I slipped into a doorway and stood there listening.

Back when I was young, I was small and wiry and stupid enough to crawl through Viet Cong tunnels looking for bad guys. I had nightmares about that experience for years.

Somewhere in this pile of rock was at least one person, perhaps more. But where?

The old fort was quiet as a tomb. Just when I thought there was nothing to hear, I heard something . . . a scratching . . .

I examined the courtyard again. There, on a second-story window ledge, a bird.

It flew.

I hung the rifle over my shoulder on its sling and got out my knife. With the knife in my right hand, cutting edge up, I began exploring.

The old fort had some modern sleeping quarters, cooking facilities, and meeting rooms. There were electric lights plugged into wall sockets. In one of the lower rooms I found a gasoline-powered generator. Forty gallons of gasoline in plastic five-gallon cans sat in the next room.

In a tower on the top floor, in a room with a magnificent view through glass windows, sat a first-class, state-of-the-art shortwave radio. I had seen the antenna as I walked toward the fort: It was on the roof above this room. I was examining the radio, wondering if I should try to disable it, when I heard a nearby door slam.

Scurrying to the door of the room, I stood frozen, listening with my ear close to the wall.

The other person in the fort was making no attempt to be quiet, which made me feel better. He obviously thought he was very much alone. And it was just one person, close, right down the hallway.

Try as I might, I could only hear the one person, a man, opening and closing drawers, scooting something—a chair probably—across a stone floor, now slamming another door shut.

Even as I watched he came out of one of the doors and walked away from me to the stairs I had used coming up. Good thing I didn't open the door to look into his room!

I got a glimpse of him crossing the courtyard, going toward the gasoline generator.

Unwilling to move, I stood there until I heard the generator start. The hum of the gasoline engine settled into a steady drone. A lightbulb above the table upon which the radio sat illuminated.

I trotted down the hallway to the room the man had come out of. I eased the door open and glanced in. Empty.

The next room was also a bedroom, also empty, so I went in and closed the door.

I was standing back from the window, watching, fifteen minutes later when the man walked out of a doorway to the courtyard almost directly opposite the room I was in, got into the Land Rover, and started it.

He drove out through the open gate trailing a wispy plume of dust. I went to another window, an outside one, and waited. In a moment I got a glimpse of the Land Rover on the road to the airport.

In the courtyard against one wall stood a water tank on legs, with plastic lines leading away to the kitchen area. I opened the fill cap and looked in. I estimated the tank contained fifty gallons of water. Apparently people using this facility brought water with them, poured it into this tank, then used it sparingly.

I stood in the courtyard looking at the water tank, cursing under my breath. The best way to kill these people would be to poison their water with some kind of delayed-action poison that would take twenty-four hours to work, so everyone would have an opportunity to ingest some. Julie Giraud could have fucked a chemist and got us some poison. I should have thought of the water tank.

Too late now.

Damn!

Before I had a chance to cuss very much, I heard a jet. The engine noise was rapidly getting louder. I dived for cover.

Seconds later a jet airplane went right over the fort, less than a hundred feet above the radio antenna.

Staying low, I scurried up the staircase to the top of the ramparts and took a look. A small passenger jet was circling to land at the airport.

I double-timed down the staircase and hotfooted it out the gate and along the trail leading to the path down to the oasis, keeping my eye on the sky in case another jet should appear.

It took me about half an hour to get back to the oasis, and another fifteen minutes to reach the place where Julie was waiting in the Humvee. Of course I didn't just charge right up to the Humvee. Still well out of sight of the vehicle, I stopped, lay down, and caught my breath.

When I quit blowing, I circled the area where the Humvee should have been, came at it from the east. At first I didn't see her. I could see the vehicle, but she wasn't in sight.

I settled down to wait.

Another jet went over, apparently slowing to land on the other side of the ridge.

A half hour passed, then another. The temperature was rising quickly, the sun climbing the sky.

Finally, Julie moved.

She was lying at the base of a bush a hundred feet from the vehicle and she had an M-16 in her hands.

Okay.

Julie Giraud was a competent pilot and acted like she had all her shit in one sock when we were planning this mission, but I wanted to see how she handled herself on the ground. If we made a mistake in Europe, we might wind up in prison. A mistake here would cost us our lives.

I crawled forward on my stomach, taking my time, just sifting along.

It took me fifteen minutes to crawl up behind her. Finally I reached out with the barrel of the Model 70, touched her foot. She spun around as if she had been stung.

I grinned at her.

"You bastard," Julie Giraud said.

"Don't you forget it, lady."

FIVE

Blowing up the fort was an impractical idea and always had been. When Julie Giraud first mentioned destroying the fort with the bad guys inside, back in Van Nuys, I had let her talk. I didn't think she had any idea how much explosives would be necessary to demolish a large stone structure, and she didn't. When I finally asked her how much C-4 she thought it would take, she looked at me blankly.

We had brought a hundred pounds of the stuff, all we could transport efficiently.

I used the binoculars to follow the third plane through the sky until it disappeared behind the ridge. It was some kind of small, twin-engined bizjet.

"How come these folks are early?" I asked her.

"I don't know."

"Your CIA friend didn't tip you off about the time switch?"

"No."

The fact these people were arriving a day early bothered me and I considered it from every angle.

Life is full of glitches and unexpected twists—who ever has a day that goes as planned? To succeed at anything you must be adaptable and flexible, and smart enough to know when backing off is the right thing to do.

I wondered just how smart I was. Should we back off?

I drove the Humvee toward the cliff where we had the Osprey parked. The land rolled, with here and there gulleys cut by the runoff from rare desert storms. These gulleys had steep sides, loose sand bottoms, and were choked with desert plants. Low places had brush and cacti, but mainly the terrain was dirt with occasional rock outcroppings. One got the impression that at some time in the geologic past the dirt had blown in, covering a stark, highly eroded landscape. I tried to keep off the exposed places as much as possible and drove very slowly to keep from raising dust.

Every so often I stopped the vehicle, got out, and listened for airplanes. Two more jets went over that I heard. That meant there were at least five jets at that desert strip, maybe more.

Julie sat silently, saying nothing as we drove along. When I killed the engine and got out to listen, she stayed in her seat.

I stopped the Humvee in a brushy draw about a mile

from the Osprey, reached for the Model 70, then snagged a canteen and hung it over my shoulder.

"May I come with you?" she asked.

"Sure."

We stopped when we got to a low rise where we could see the V-22 and the area around it. I looked everything over with binoculars, then settled down at the base of a green bush that resembled greasewood, trying to get what shade there was. The temperature must have been ninety by that time.

"Aren't we going down to the plane?"

"It's safer here."

Julie picked another bush and crawled under.

I was silently complimenting her on her ability to accept direction without question or explanation when she said, "You don't take many chances, do you?"

"I try not to."

"So you're just going to kill these people, then get on with the rest of your life?"

I took a good look at her face. "If you're going to chicken out," I said, "do it now, so I don't have to lie here sweating the program for the whole damned day."

"I'm not going to chicken out. I just wondered if you were."

"You said these people were terrorists, had blown up airliners. That still true?"

"Absolutely."

"Then I won't lose any sleep over them." I shifted around, got comfortable, kept the rifle just under my hands.

She met my eyes, and apparently decided this point needed a little more exploring. "I'm killing them because they killed my parents. You're killing them for money."

I sighed, tossed her the binoculars.

"Every few minutes, glass the area around the plane, then up on the ridge," I told her. "Take your time, look at everything in your field of view, look for movement. Any kind of movement. And don't let the sun glint off the binoculars."

"How are we going to do it?" she asked as she stared through the glasses.

"Blowing the fort was a pipe dream, as you well know."

She didn't reply, just scanned with the binoculars.

"The best way to do it is to blow up the planes with the people on them."

A grin crossed her face, then disappeared.

I rolled over, arranged the rifle just so, and settled down for a nap. I was so tired.

The sun had moved a good bit by the time I awakened. The air was stifling, with no detectable breeze. Julie was stretched out asleep, the binoculars in front of her. I used the barrel of the rifle to hook the strap and lift them, bring them over to me without making noise.

The land was empty, dead. Not a single creature stirred, not even a bird. The magnified images I could see through the binoculars shimmered in the heat.

Finally I put the thing down, sipped at the water in my canteen.

South Africa. Soon. Maybe I'd become a diamond prospector. There was a whole lot of interesting real estate in South Africa, or so I'd heard, and I intended to see it. Get a jeep and some camping gear and head out.

Julie's crack about killing for money rankled, of course. The fact was that these people were terrorists, predators who preyed on the weak and defenseless. They had blown up an airliner. Take money for killing them? Yep. And glad to get it, too.

Julie had awakened and moved off into the brush out of sight to relieve herself when I spotted a man on top of the cliff, a few hundred yards to the right of the Osprey. I picked him up as I swept the top of the cliff with the binoculars.

I turned the focus wheel, tried to sharpen the dancing image. Too much heat.

It was a man, all right. Standing there with a rifle on a sling over his shoulder, surveying the desert with binoculars. Instinctively I backed up a trifle, ensured the binoculars were in shade so there would be no sun reflections off the glass or frame. And I glanced at the airplane.

It should be out of sight of the man due to the way the cliff outcropped between his position and the plane. I hoped. In any event he wasn't looking at it.

I gritted my teeth, studied his image, tried by sheer strength of will to make it steadier in the glass. The distance between us was about six hundred yards, I estimated.

I put down the binoculars and slowly brought up the Model 70. I had a variable power scope on it which I habitually kept cranked to maximum magnification. The figure of the man leaped at me through the glass.

I put the crosshairs on his chest, studied him. Even through the shimmering air I could see the cloth he wore on his head and the headband that held it in place. He was wearing light-colored trousers and a shirt. And he was holding binoculars pointed precisely at me.

I heard a rustle behind me.

"Freeze, Julie," I said, loud enough that she would plainly hear me.

She stopped.

I kept the scope on him, flicked off the safety. I had automatically assumed a shooting position when I raised the rifle. Now I wiggled my left elbow into the hard earth, settled the rifle in tighter against my shoulder.

He just stood there, looking right at us.

I only saw him because he was silhouetted on the skyline. In the shade under this brush we should be invisible to him. Should be.

Now he was scanning the horizon again. Since I had been watching he had not once looked down at the foot of the cliff upon which he was standing.

He was probably a city soldier, I decided. Hadn't been

trained to look close first, before he scanned terrain farther away.

After another long moment he turned away, began
walking slowly along the top of the cliff to my right, away
from the Osprey. I kept the crosshairs of the scope on
him until he was completely out of sight. Only then did
I put the safety back on and lower the rifle.

"You can come in now," I said.

She crawled back under her bush.

"Did you see him?" I asked.

"Yes. Did he see the airplane?"

"I'm certain he didn't."

"How did he miss it?"

"It was just a little out of sight, I think. Even if he
could have seen it, he never really looked in the right
direction."

"We were lucky," she said.

I grunted. It was too hot to discuss philosophy. I lay
there under my bush wondering just how crazy ol' Julie
Giraud really was.

"If he had seen the plane, Charlie Dean, would you
have shot him?"

What a question!

"You're damned right," I muttered, more than a little
disgusted. "If he had seen the plane, I would have shot
him and piled you into the cockpit and made you get us
the hell out of here before all the Indians in the world
showed up to help with the pleasant chore of lifting our
hair. These guys are playing for keeps, lady. You and me

had better be on the same sheet of music or we will be well and truly fucked."

Every muscle in her face tensed. "We're not leaving," she snarled, "until those sons of bitches are dead. All of them. Every last one."

She was over the edge.

A wave of cold fear swept over me. It was bad enough being on the edge of a shooting situation; now my backup was around the bend. If she went down or freaked out, how in the hell was I going to get off this rock pile?

"I've been trying to decide," she continued, "if you really have the balls for this, Charlie Dean, or if you're going to turn tail on me when crunch time comes and run like a rabbit. You're old: You look old, you sound old. Maybe you had the balls years ago, maybe you don't anymore."

From the leg pocket of her flight suit she pulled a small automatic, a .380 from the looks of it. She held it where I could see it, pointed it more or less in my direction. "Grow yourself another set of balls, Charlie Dean. Nobody is running out."

I tossed her the binoculars. "Call me if they come back," I said. I put the rifle beside me and lay down.

Sure, I thought about what a dumb ass I was. Three million bucks!—I was going to have to earn every damned dollar.

Hoo boy.

Okay, I'll admit it: I knew she was crazy that first day in Van Nuys.

I made a conscious effort to relax. The earth was

warm, the air was hot, and I was exhausted. I was asleep in nothing flat.

The sun was about to set when I awoke. My binoculars were on the sand beside me and Julie Giraud was nowhere in sight. I used the scope on the rifle to examine the Osprey and the cliff behind it.

I spotted her in seconds, moving around under the plane. No one else visible.

While we had a little light, I went back for the Humvee. I crawled up on it, taking my time, ensuring that no one was there waiting for me.

When we left it that morning we had piled some dead brush on the hood and top of the vehicle, so I pulled that off before I climbed in.

Taking it slow so I wouldn't raise dust, I drove the mile or so to the Osprey. I got there just as the last rays of the sun vanished.

I backed up to the trailer and we attached it to the Humvee.

"Want to tell me your plan, Charlie Dean?" she asked. "Or do you have one?"

As I repacked the contents of the trailer I told her how I wanted to do it. Amazingly, she agreed readily.

She was certainly hard to figure. One minute I thought she was a real person, complete with a conscience and the intellectual realization that even the enemy were human beings, then the next second she was a female Rambo, ready to gut them all, one by one.

She helped me make up C-4 bombs, rig the detonators and radio controls. I did the first one, she watched intently, then she did one on her own. I checked it, and she got everything right.

"Don't take any unnecessary chances tonight," I said. "I want you alive and well when this is over so you can fly me out of here."

She merely nodded. It was impossible to guess what she might have been thinking.

I wasn't about to tell her that I had flown helicopters in Vietnam. I was never a rated pilot, but I was young and curious, so the pilots often let me practice under their supervision. I had watched her with the Osprey and thought that I could probably fly it if absolutely necessary. The key would be to use the checklist and take plenty of time. If I could get it started, I thought I could fly it out. There were parachutes in the thing, so I would not need to land it.

I didn't say any of this to her, of course.

We had a packet of radio receivers and detonators—I counted them—enough for six bombs. If I set them all on the same frequency I could blow up six planes with one push of the button. If I could get the bombs aboard six planes without being discovered.

What if there were more than six planes? Well, I had some pyrotechnic fuses, which seemed impractical to use on an airplane, and some chemical fuses. In the cargo bay of the Osprey I examined the chemical fuses by flashlight. Eight hours seemed to be the maximum setting.

The problem was that I didn't know when the bad guys planned to leave.

As I was meditating on fuses and bombs, I went outside and walked around the Osprey. There was a turreted three-barreled fifty-caliber machine gun in the nose of the thing. Air Force Ospreys didn't carry stingers like this, but this one belonged to the Marine Corps, or did until twenty-four hours ago.

I opened the service bay. Gleaming brass in the feed trays reflected the dim evening light.

Julie was standing right behind me. "I stole this one because it had the gun," she remarked. "Less range than the Air Force birds, but the gun sold me."

"Maximum firepower is always a good choice."

"What are you thinking?" she asked.

We discussed contingencies as we wired up the transfer pump in the bladder fuel tank we had chained down in the cargo bay. We used the aircraft's battery to power the pump, so all we had to do was watch as three thousand pounds of jet fuel was transferred into the aircraft's tanks.

My plan had bombs, bullets, and a small river of blood—we hoped—just the kind of tale that appealed to Julie Giraud. She even allowed herself a tight smile.

Me? I had a cold knot in the pit of my stomach and I was sweating.

SIX

We finished loading the Humvee and the trailer attached to it before sunset and ate MREs in the twilight.
As soon as it was dark, we donned our night-vision goggles and drove toward the oasis. I stopped often to get up
on the vehicle's hood, the best vantage point around, and
take a squint in all directions.

I parked the vehicle at the foot of the trail. "If I'm not
back in an hour and a half, they've caught me," I told
Julie Giraud. I smeared my face with grease to cut the
white shine, checked my reflection in the rearview mirror, then did my neck and the back of my hands.

"If they catch you," she said, "I won't pay you the rest
of the money."

"Women are too maudlin to be good soldiers," I told

her. "You've got to stop this cloying sentimentality. Save the tears for the twenty-five-year reunion."

When I was as invisible as I was going to get, I hoisted a rucksack that I had packed that evening, put the M-16 over my shoulder, and started up the trail.

Every now and then I switched the goggles from ambient light to infrared and looked for telltale heat sources. I spotted some small mammal, too small to be human. I continued up the ridge, wondering how any critters managed to make a living in this godforsaken desert.

The temperature had dropped significantly from the high during the afternoon. I estimated the air was still at eighty degrees, but it would soon go below seventy. Even the earth was cooling, although not as quickly as the air.

I topped the ridge slowly, on the alert for security patrols. Before we committed ourselves to a course of action, we had to know how many security people were prowling around.

No one in sight now.

I got off to one side of the trail, just in case, and walked toward the old fortress, the Camel. Tonight light shone from several of the structure's windows, light visible for many miles in that clean desert air.

I was still at least five hundred yards from the walls when I first heard the hum of the generator, barely audible at that distance. The noise gradually increased as I approached the structure. When I was about fifty yards from the wall, I circled the fort to a vantage point where

I could see the main gate, the gate where I entered on my last visit. It was standing open. A guard with an assault rifle sat on a stool near the gate; he was quite clear in the goggles. He was sitting under an overhang of the wall at a place where he could watch the road that led off the ridge, the road to the oasis and the airfield. He was not wearing any night-vision aid, just sitting in the darkness under the wall.

The drone of the gasoline generator meant that he could hear nothing. Of course, it handicapped me as well.

I continued around the structure, crossing the road at a spot out of sight of the man at the gate. Taking my time, slipping through the sparse brush as carefully as possible, I inspected every foot of the wall. The main gate was the only entrance I noticed on my first visit, yet I wanted to be sure.

A man strolled on top of the wall on the side opposite the main gate; the instant I saw him I dropped motionless to the ground. Seconds passed as he continued to walk, then finally he reversed his course. When he disappeared from view I scurried over to a rock outcrop and crouched under it, with my body out of sight from the wall.

If he had an infrared scope or any kind of ambient light collector, he could have seen me lying on the open ground.

I crouched there waiting for something to happen. If they came streaming out of the main gate, they could trap me on the point of this ridge, hunt me down at their leisure.

As I waited I discovered that the M-16 was already in my hands. I had removed it from my shoulder automatically, without thinking.

Several minutes passed as I waited, listening to the hypnotic drone of the generator, waiting for something to happen. Anything.

Finally a head became visible on top of the wall. The sentry again, still strolling aimlessly. He leaned against the wall for a while, then disappeared.

Now I hurried along, completed my circumnavigation of the fort.

I saw only the two men, one on the gate and the man who had been walking the walls. Although I had seen the man on the wall twice, I was convinced it was the same person. And I was certain there was only one entrance to the fort, the main gate.

I had to go through that gate so I was going to have to take out the guard. I was going to have to do it soon, then hope I could get in and out before his absence from his post was noticed or someone came to relieve him. Taking chances like that wasn't the best way to live to spend that three million dollars, that's for sure, but we didn't have the time or resources to minimize the risk. I was going to have to have some luck here or we had no chance to pull off this thing.

This whole goddamn expedition was half-baked, I reflected, and certainly no credit to me. Man, why didn't I think of poisoning their water supply when we were brainstorming in Germany?

In my favor was the fact that these people didn't seem very worried about their safety or anything else. A generator snoring away, only two guards? An open gate?

I worked my way to the wall, then turned and crept toward the guard. The generator hid the sounds I made as I crept along. He was facing the road.

I got about ten feet from him and froze. He was facing away from me at a slight angle, but if I tried to get closer, he was going to pick me up in his peripheral vision. I sensed it, so I froze.

He changed his position on the stool, played with the rifle on his knees, looked at the myriad of stars that hung just over our heads. Finally he stood and stretched. For an instant he turned away from me. I covered the distance in two bounds, wrapped my arm around his mouth, and jammed my knife into his back up to the hilt.

The knife went between his ribs right into his heart. Two convulsive tremors, then he was dead.

I carried him and his rifle off into the darkness. He weighed maybe one-eighty, as near as I could tell.

One of the outcroppings that formed the edge of the top of the ridge would keep him hidden from anyone but a determined searcher. After I stashed the body, I hurried back to the gate. I took off my night-vision goggles, waited for my eyes to adjust. I took off my rifle, leaned it against the wall out of sight.

As I waited I saw the man on the ramparts walking his rounds. He was in no hurry, obviously bored. I got a radio-controlled bomb from the rucksack, checked the frequency, and turned on the receiver.

The Land Rover was in the courtyard. When the man on the wall was out of sight, I slipped over to it and lay down. I pulled out the snap wire and snapped it around one of the suspension arms. The antenna of the bomb I let dangle.

This little job took less than thirty seconds. Then I scurried across the courtyard into the shelter of the stair-case.

The conferees were probably in the living area; I sure as hell hoped they were. My edge was that the people here were not on alert. And why should they be? This fort was buried in the most desolate spot on the planet, hundreds of miles from anyplace.

Still, my life was on the line, so I moved as cautiously as I could, trying very hard to make no noise at all, pausing to listen carefully before I rounded any corner. My progress was glacial. It took me almost five minutes to climb the stairs and inch down the corridor to the radio room.

The hum of the generator was muted the farther away from it I moved, but it was the faint background noise that covered any minor noise I was making. And any minor noise anyone else was making. That reality had me sweating.

The door to the radio room was ajar, the room dark.

Knocking out the generator figured to be the easiest way to disable the radio, unless they had a battery to use as backup. I was betting they did.

After listening for almost a minute outside the door, I eased it open gently, my fighting knife in my hand.

The only light came through the interior window from the floods in the courtyard. The room was empty of people!

I went in fast, laid my knife on the table, got a bomb out of the rucksack. This one was rigged with a chemical fuse, so I broke the chemicals, shook the thing to start the reaction, then put the package—explosive, detonator, fuse, and all—directly behind the radio. As I turned I was struck in the face by a runaway Freightliner.

Only partially conscious, I found myself falling. A rough hand gripped me fiercely, then another truck slammed into my face. If I hadn't turned my head to protect myself, that blow would have put me completely out.

As it was, I couldn't stay upright. My legs turned to jelly and I went to the floor, which was cold and hard.

"What a pleasant surprise," my assailant said in highly accented English, then kicked me in the side. His boot almost broke my left arm, which was fortunate, because if he had managed to get a clean shot at my ribs he would have caved in a lung.

I wasn't feeling very lucky just then. My arm felt like it was in four pieces and my side was on fire. I fought for air.

I couldn't take much more of this. If I didn't do something pretty damned quick he was going to kick me to death.

Curling into a fetal position, I used my right hand to

draw my hideout knife from my left boot. I had barely got it out when he kicked me in the kidney.

At first I thought the guy had rammed a knife into my back—the pain was that intense. I was fast running out of time.

I rolled over toward him, just in time to meet his foot coming in again. I slashed with the knife, which had a razor-sharp two-sided blade about three inches long. I felt it bite into something.

He stepped back then, bent down to feel his calf. I got my feet under me and rose into a crouch.

"A knife, is it? You think you can save yourself with that?"

While he was talking he lashed out again with a leg. It was a kick designed to distract me, tempt me to go for his leg again with the knife.

I didn't, so when he spun around and sent another of those iron-fisted artillery shots toward my head, I was ready. I went under the incoming punch and slashed his stomach with the knife.

I cut him bad.

Now he grunted in pain, sagged toward the radio table.

I gathered myself, got out of his way, got into a crouch so I could defend myself.

He was holding his stomach with both hands. In the dim light I could see blood. I had really gotten him.

"Shouldn't have played with you," he said, and reached for the pistol in the holster on his belt.

Too late. I was too close. With one mighty swing of

my arm I slashed his throat. Blood spewed out, a look of surprise registered on his face, then he collapsed.

Blood continued to pump from his neck.

I had to wipe the sweat from my eyes.

Jesus! My hands were shaking, trembling.

Never again, God! I promise. Never again!

I stowed the little knife back in my boot, retrieved the rucksack and my fighting knife from the table.

Outside in the corridor I carefully pulled the door to the radio room shut, made sure it latched.

Down the stairs, across the courtyard, through the gate. Safe in the darkness outside, I retrieved my M-16 and puked up my MREs.

Yeah, I'm a real tough guy. Shit!

Then I trotted for the trail to the oasis. It wasn't much of a trot. My side, back, and arm were on fire, and my face was still numb. The best I could manage was a hell-bent staggering gait.

As I ran the numbness in my side and back wore off. I wheezed like an old horse and savored the pain, which was proof positive I was still alive.

Julie Giraud was standing beside the Humvee chewing her fingernails. I took my time looking over the area, made sure she was really alone, then walked the last hundred feet.

"Hey," I said.

My voice made her jump. She glanced at my face, then stared. "What happened?"

I eased myself into the driver's seat.

"A guy was waiting for me."

"What?"

"He spoke to me in English."

"Well . . ."

"Didn't even try a phrase in Arabic. Just spoke to me in English."

"You're bleeding under your right eye, I think. With all that grease it's hard to tell."

"Pay attention to what I'm telling you. He spoke to me in English. He knew I understood it. Doesn't that worry you?"

"What about the radio?"

"He knew I was coming. Someone told him. He was waiting for me."

"You're just guessing."

"He almost killed me."

"He didn't."

"If they knew we were coming, we're dead."

Before I could draw another breath, she had a pistol pointed at me. She placed the muzzle against the side of my head.

"I'll tell you one more time, Charlie Dean, one more time. These people are baby-killers, murderers of women and kids and old people. They have been tried in a court of law and found guilty. We are going to kill them so they can never kill again."

Crazy! She was crazy as hell!

Her voice was low, every word distinctly pronounced: "I don't care what they know or who told them what. *We are going to kill these men. You will help me do it or*

I will kill you. Have I made it plain enough? Do you un-derstand?"

"Did the court sentence these people to die?" I asked.

"*I* sentenced them! *Me!* Julie Giraud. And I am going to carry it out. *Death.* For every one of them."

SEVEN

The satellite photos showed a wash just off the east end of the runway. We worked our way along it, then crawled to a spot that allowed us to look the length of it.

The runway was narrow, no more than fifty feet wide. The planes were parked on a mat about halfway down. The wind was out of the west, as it usually was at night. To take off, the planes would have to taxi individually to the east end of the runway, this end, turn around, then take off to the west.

"If they don't discover that the guards are missing, search the place, find the bombs and disable them, we've got a chance," I said. "Just a chance."

"You're a pessimist."

"You got that right."

"How many guards do you think are around the planes?"

"I don't know. All of the pilots could be there; there could easily be a dozen people down there."

"So we just sneak over, see what's what?"

"That's about the size of it."

"For three million dollars I thought I was getting someone who knew how to pull this off."

"And I thought the person hiring me was sane. We both made a bad deal. You want to fly the Osprey back to Germany and tell them you're sorry you borrowed it?"

"They didn't kill your parents."

"I guarantee you, before this is over you're going to be elbow-deep in blood, lady. And your parents will still be dead."

"You said that before."

"It's still true."

I was tempted to give the bitch a rifle and send her down the runway to do her damnedest, but I didn't.

I took the goddamn M-16, adjusted the night-vision goggles, and went myself. My left side hurt like hell, from my shoulder to my hip. I flexed my arm repeatedly, trying to work the pain out.

The planes were readily visible with the goggles. I kept to the waist-high brush on the side of the runway toward the planes, which were parked in a row. It wasn't until I got about halfway there that I could count them. Six planes.

The idea was to get the terrorists into the planes, then destroy the planes in the air. The last thing we wanted was the terrorists and the guards out here in this desert running around looking for us. With dozens of them and only two of us, there was only one way for that tale to end.

No, we needed to get them into the planes. I didn't have enough radio-controlled detonators to put on all the planes, so I thought if I could disable some of the planes and put bombs on the rest, we would have a chance. But first we had to eliminate the guards.

If the flight crews were bivouacked near the planes, this was going to get really dicey.

I took my time, went slowly from bush to bush, looking at everything. When I used infrared, I could see a heat source to the south of the planes that had to be an open fire. No people, though.

I was crouched near the main wheel of the plane on the end of the mat when I saw my first guard. He was relieving himself against the nearest airplane's nose-wheel.

When he finished he zipped up and resumed his stroll along the mat.

I went behind the plane and made my way toward the fire.

They had built the thing in a fifty-five-gallon drum. Two people stood with their backs to the fire, warming up. I could have used a stretch by that fire myself: The temperature was below sixty degrees by that time and going lower.

No tents. No one in sleeping bags that I could see.

Three of them.

I settled down to wait. Before we made a move, I had to be certain of the number of people that were here and where they were. If I missed one I wouldn't live to spend a dollar of Julie Giraud's blood money.

Lying there in the darkness, I tried to figure it all out. Didn't get anywhere. Why that guy addressed me in English I had no idea. He was certainly no Englishman; nor was he a native of any English-speaking country.

Julie Giraud wanted these sons of the desert dead and in hell—of that I was absolutely convinced. She wasn't a good enough actress to fake it. The money she had paid me was real enough, the V-22 Osprey was real, the guns were real, the bombs were real, we were so deep in the desert we could never drive or hike out. Never.

She was my ticket out. If she went down, I was going to have to try to fly the Osprey myself. If the plane was damaged, we were going to die here.

Simple as that.

Right then I wished to hell I was back in Van Nuys in the filling station watching Candy make change. I was too damned old for this shit and I knew it.

I had been lying in the dirt for about an hour when the guy walking the line came to the fire and one of the loafers there went into the darkness to replace him. The two at the fire then crawled into sleeping bags.

I waited another half hour, using the goggles to keep track of the sentry.

The sentry was first. I was crouched in the bushes when he came over less than six feet from me, dropped his trousers, and squatted.

I left him there with his pants around his ankles and went over to the sleeping bags. Both the sleeping men died without making a sound.

Killing them wasn't heroic or glorious or anything like that. I felt dirty, coated with the kind of slime that would never wash off. The fact that they would have killed me just as quickly if they had had the chance didn't make it any easier. They killed for political reasons, I killed for money: We were the same kind of animal.

I walked back down the runway to where Julie Giraud waited.

I got into the Humvee without saying anything and started the motor.

"How many were there?" she asked.

"Three," I said.

We placed radio-controlled bombs in three of the airplanes. We taped a bomb securely in the nosewheel well of each of them, then dangled the antennas outside, so they would hang out the door even if the wheels were retracted.

When we were finished with that we stood for a moment in the darkness discussing things. The fort was over a mile away and I prayed the generator was still running, making fine background music. Julie crawled under the first plane and looked it over. First she fired shots into the nose tires, which began hissing. Then she fired a bullet into the bottom of each wing tank. Fuel ran out and soaked into the dirt.

There was little danger in this, as Julie well knew. The tanks would not explode unless something very hot went into a mixture of fuel vapor and oxygen: She was putting a bullet into liquid. The biggest danger was that the low-powered pistol bullets would fail to penetrate the metal skin of the wing and the fuel tank. In fact, she fired six shots into the tanks of the second plane before she was satisfied with the amount of fuel running out on the ground.

When she had flattened the nose tires of all of the unbooby-trapped planes and punched bullet holes in the tanks, she walked over to the Humvee, reeking of jet fuel.

"Let's go," she said grimly.

As we drove away I glanced at her. She was smiling.

For the first time, I began to seriously worry that she would intentionally leave me in the desert.

I comforted myself with the fact that she didn't really care about the money she was going to owe me. She could justify the deaths of these men, but if she killed me, she was no better than they.

I hoped she saw it that way, too.

She let me out of the Humvee on the road about a quarter of a mile below the fort. From where I stood the road rose steadily and curved through three switchbacks until it reached the main gate.

With my Model 70 in hand, I left the road and began climbing the hill straight toward the main gate. The night was about over. Even as I climbed I thought I could see the sky beginning to lighten up in the east.

The generator was off. No light or sound came from the massive old fort, which was now a dark presence that blotted out the stars above me.

Were they in bed?

The gate was still open, with no one in sight on top of the wall or in the courtyard. That was a minor miracle or an invitation to a fool—me. If they had discovered King Kong's body they were going to be waiting.

I stood there in the darkness listening to the silence, trying to convince myself these guys were all in their beds sound asleep, that the miracle was real.

No guts, no glory, I told myself, sucked it up, and slipped through the gate. I sifted my way past the Land Rover and began climbing the stairs.

I didn't go up those stairs slow as sap in a maple tree this time. I zipped up the steps, knife in one hand and pistol in the other. Maybe I just didn't care. If they killed me, maybe that would be a blessing.

The corridor on top was empty, and the door to the radio shack was still closed. I eased it open and peeked in. King Kong was still lying in a pool of his own blood on the floor, just the way I had left him.

I pulled the door shut, then tiptoed along the corridor toward an alcove overlooking the courtyard.

I heard a noise and crouched in the darkness.

Someone snoring.

The sound was coming from an open door on my left. At least two men.

I eased past the door, moving as quietly as I could, until I reached the alcove.

Nothing stirred in the quiet moment before dawn.

From the rucksack hanging from my shoulder I removed three hand grenades, placed them on the floor near my feet.

And I waited.

EIGHT

Dawn took its own sweet time arriving. I was sore, stiff, hungry, and I loathed myself. I was also so exhausted that I was having trouble thinking clearly. What was there about Julie that scared me?

It wasn't that she might kill me or leave me stranded in the desert surrounded by corpses. She didn't strike me as the kind to double-cross anyone: If I was wrong about that I was dead and that was that. There was something else, something that didn't fit, but tired as I was, I couldn't put my finger on it.

She stole the V-22, hired me to help her . . .

Well, we would make it or we wouldn't.

I sat with my rifle on my lap, finger on the trigger,

leaned back against the wall, closed my eyes just for a moment. I was so tired . . .

I awakened with a jerk. Somewhere in the fort a door closed with a minor bang.

The day was here, the sun was shining straight in through the openings in the wall.

Someone was moving around. Another door slammed.

I looked at my watch. The bombs should have gone off twenty minutes ago. I had been asleep over an hour.

I slowly rose from the floor on which I had been sitting, so stiff and sore I could hardly move. I picked up the grenades and pocketed them. Moving as carefully and quietly as I could, I got up on the railing, put my leg up to climb onto the roof.

The rifle slipped off my shoulder. I grabbed for the strap and was so sore I damn near dropped it.

The courtyard was thirty feet below. I teetered on the railing, the rifle hanging by a strap from my right forearm, the rucksack dangling, every muscle I owned screaming in protest.

Then I was safely up, pulling all that damn gear along with me.

Taking my time, I spread out the gear, got out the grenades, and placed them where I could easily reach them.

I took a long drink from my canteen, then screwed the lid back on and put it away.

The radio that controlled the bombs was not large. I set the frequency very carefully, turned the thing on, and let the capacitor charge. When the green light came on, I gingerly set the radio aside.

Three minutes later, a muffled bang from the bomb behind the shortwave radio slapped the air.

I lay down on the roof and gripped the rifle.

Running feet.

Shouts. Shouts in Arabic.

It didn't take them long to zero in on the radio room. I heard running feet, several men, pounding along the corridor.

They didn't spend much time in there looking at the remains of King Kong or the shortwave. More shouts rang through the building.

Julie Giraud and I had argued about what would happen next. I predicted that these guys would panic, would soon decide that the logical, best course of action was a fast plane ride back to civilization. I suspected they were bureaucrats at heart, string-pullers. Julie thought they might be warriors, that their first instinct would be to fight. We would soon see who was right.

I could hear the voices bubbling out of the courtyard, then what sounded like orders given in a clean, calm voice. That would never do. I pulled the pin from a grenade, then threw it at the wall on the other side of the courtyard.

The grenade struck the wall, made a noise that attracted the attention of the people below, then exploded just before it hit the ground.

A scream. Moans.

I tossed a second grenade, enjoyed the explosion, then hustled along the rooftop. I lay down beside a chimney in a place that allowed me to watch the rest of the roof and the area just beyond the main gate.

From here I could also see the planes parked on the airfield, gleaming brightly in the morning sun.

Someone stuck his head over the edge of the roof. He was gone too quick for me to get around, but I figured he would pop up again with a weapon of some kind, so I got the Model 70 pointed and flicked off the safety. Sure enough, fifteen seconds later the head popped back up and I squeezed off a shot. His body hit the pavement thirty feet below with a heavy plop.

The Land Rover could not carry them all, of course. Still, I thought this crowd would go for it as if it were a lifeboat on the *Titanic*. I was not surprised to hear the engine start even though I had tossed two grenades into the courtyard where the vehicle was parked: The Rover was essentially impervious to shrapnel damage, and should run for a bit, at least, as long as the radiator remained intact.

Angry shouts reached me. Apparently the Rover driver refused to wait for a full load.

I kept my head down, waited until I heard the Rover clear the gate and start down the road. Then I pushed the button on the radio control.

The explosion was quite satisfying. In about half a minute a column of smoke from the wreckage could be seen from where I lay.

I stayed put. I was in a good defensive position, what happened next was up to the crowd below.

The sun climbed higher in the sky and on the roof of that old fort, the temperature soared. I was sweating pretty good by then, was exhausted and hungry . . . Finally I had had enough. I crawled over to one of the cooking chimneys and stood up.

They were going down the road in knots of threes and fours. With the binoculars I counted them. Twenty-eight.

There was no way to know if that was all of them.

Crouching, I made my way to the courtyard side, where I could look down in, and listen.

No sound but the wind, which was out of the west at about fifteen knots, a typical desert day this time of year.

After a couple minutes of this, I inched my head over the edge for a look. Three bodies lay sprawled in the court-yard.

I had a fifty-foot rope in the rucksack. I tied one end around a chimney and tossed it over the wall on the side away from the main gate. Then I clambered over.

Safely on the ground, I kept close to the wall, out of sight of the openings above me. On the north side the edge of the ridge was close, about forty yards. I got opposite that point, gripped my rifle with both hands, and ran for it.

No shots.

Safely under the ledge, I sat down, caught my breath, and had a drink of water.

If there was anyone still in the fort waiting to ambush me, he could wait until doomsday for all I cared.

I moved downslope and around the ridge about a hundred yards to a place where I could see the runway and the airplanes and the road.

The figures were still distinct in my binoculars, walking briskly.

What would they do when they got to the airplanes? They would find the bodies of three men who died violently and three sabotaged airplanes. Three of the airplanes would appear to be intact.

The possibility that the intact airplanes were sabotaged would of course occur to them. I argued that they would not get in those planes, but would hunker down and wait until some of their friends came looking for them. Of course, the only food and water they had would be in the planes or what they had carried from the fort, but they could comfortably sit tight for a couple of days.

We couldn't. If the Libyan military found us, the Osprey would be MiG-meat and we would be doomed.

A thorough, careful preflight of the bizjets would turn up the bombs, of course. We needed to panic these people, not give them the time to search the jets or find holes to crawl into.

Panic was Julie's job.

She had grinned when I told her how she would have to do it.

I used the binoculars to check the progress of the walking men. They were about a mile away now, approaching the mat where the airplanes were parked. The laggards were hurrying to catch up with the leaders. Apparently no one wanted to take the chance that he might be left behind.

Great outfit, that.

The head of the column had just reached the jets when I heard the Osprey. It was behind me, coming down the ridge.

In seconds it shot over the fort, which was to my left, and dived toward the runway.

Julie was a fine pilot, and the Osprey was an extraordinary machine. She kept the engines horizontal and made a high-speed pass over the bizjets, clearing the tail of the middle one by about fifty feet. I watched the whole show through my binoculars.

She gave the terrorists a good look at the U.S. Marine Corps markings on the plane.

The Osprey went out about a mile and began the transition to rotor-borne flight. I watched it slow, watched the engines tilt up, then watched it drop to just a few feet above the desert.

Julie kept the plane moving forward just fast enough to stay out of the tremendous dust cloud that the rotors kicked up, a speed of about twenty knots, I estimated.

She came slowly down the runway. Through the binoculars I saw the muzzle flashes as she squeezed off a burst from the flex Fifty. I knew she planned to shoot at one of the disabled jets, see if she could set it afire. The fuel tanks would still contain fuel vapor and oxygen, so a high-powered bullet in the right place should find something to ignite.

Swinging the binoculars to the planes, I was pleasantly surprised to see one erupt in flame.

Yep.

The Osprey accelerated. Julie rotated the engines down and climbed away.

The terrorists didn't know how many enemies they faced. Nor how many Ospreys were about. They were lightly armed and not equipped for a desert firefight, so they had limited options. Apparently that was the way they figured it, too, because in less than a minute the first jet taxied out. Another came right behind it. The third was a few seconds late, but it taxied onto the runway before the first reached the end and turned around.

The first plane had to wait for the other two. There was just room on the narrow strip for each of them to turn, but there was no pullout, no way for one plane to get out of the way of the other two. The first two had to wait until the last plane to leave the mat turned around in front of them.

Finally all three had turned and were sitting one behind the other, pointing west into the wind. The first plane rolled. Ten seconds later the second followed. The third waited maybe fifteen seconds, then it began rolling.

The first plane broke ground as Julie Giraud came screaming in from the east at a hundred feet above the ground. The Osprey looked to be flying almost flat out, which Julie said was about 270 knots.

She overtook the jets just as the third one broke ground.

She had moved a bit in front of it, still ripping along,

when the second and third plane exploded. Looking through the binoculars, it looked as if the nose came off each plane. The damaged fuselages tilted down and smashed into the ground, making surprisingly little dust when they hit.

The first plane, a Lear I think, seemed undamaged.

The bomb must have failed to explode.

The pilot of the bizjet had his wheels retracted now, was accelerating with the nose down. But not fast enough. Julie Giraud was overtaking nicely.

Through the binoculars I saw the telltale wisp of smoke from the nose of the Osprey. She was using the gun.

The Lear continued to accelerate, now began to widen the distance between it and the trailing Osprey.

"It's going to get away," I whispered. The words were just out of my mouth when the thing caught fire.

Trailing black smoke, the Lear did a slow roll over onto its back. The nose came down. The roll continued, but before the pilot could level the wings the plane smeared itself across the earth in a gout of fire and smoke.

NINE

Julie Giraud landed the Osprey on the runway near the sabotaged planes. When I walked up she was sitting in the shade under the left wing with an M-16 across her lap.

She had undoubtedly searched the area before I arrived, made sure no one had missed the plane rides to hell. Fire had spread to the other sabotaged airplanes, and now all three were burning. Black smoke tailed away on the desert wind.

"So how does it feel?" I asked as I settled onto the ground beside her.

"Damn good, thank you very much."

The heat was building, a fierce dry heat that sucked

the moisture right out of you. I got out my canteen and drained the thing.

"How do you feel?" she asked after a bit, just to be polite.

"Exhausted and dirty."

"I could use a bath, too."

"The dirty I feel ain't gonna wash off."

"That's too bad."

"I'm breaking your heart." I got to my feet. "Let's get this thing back to the cliff and covered with camouflage netting. Then we can sleep."

She nodded, got up, led the way into the machine.

We were spreading the net over the top of the plane when we heard a jet.

"Getting company," I said.

Julie was standing on top of the Osprey. Now she shaded her eyes, looked north, tried to spot the plane that we heard.

She saw it first, another bizjet. That was a relief to me—a fighter might have spotted the Osprey and strafed it.

"Help me get the net off it," she demanded, and began tossing armloads of net onto the ground.

"Are you tired of living?"

"Anyone coming to visit that crowd of baby-killers is a terrorist himself."

"So you're going to kill them?"

"If I can. Now drag that net out of my way!"

I gathered a double armful and picked it up. Julie climbed down, almost dived through the door into the machine. It took me a couple minutes to drag the net clear, and took Julie about that long to get the engines started and the plane ready to fly.

The instant I gave a thumbs-up, she applied power and lifted off.

I hid my face so I wouldn't get dirt in my eyes.

Away she went in a cloud of dirt.

She shot the plane down. The pilot landed, then tried to take off when he saw the Osprey and the burned-out jets. Julie Giraud used the flex Fifty on him and turned the jet into a fireball a hundred yards off the end of the runway.

When she landed I got busy with the net, spreading it out.

"You are the craziest goddamn broad I ever met," I told her. "You are no better than these terrorists. You're just like them."

"Bullshit," she said contemptuously.

"You don't know who the hell you just killed. For all you know you may have killed a planeload of oil-company geologists."

"Whoever it was was in the wrong place at the wrong time."

"Just like your parents."

"Somebody has to take on the predators," she shouted at me. "They feed on us. If we don't fight back, they'll eat us all."

I let her have the last word. I was sick of her and sick of me and wished to Christ I had never left Van Nuys.

. . .

I got a little sleep that afternoon in the shade under a wing, but I had too much on my mind to do more than doze. Darkness finally came and we took the net off the plane for the last time. We left the net, the Humvee, the trailer, everything. I put all the stuff we didn't need over and around the trailer as tightly as I could, then put a chemical fuse in the last of the C-4 in the trailer and set it to blow in six hours.

When we lifted off, I didn't even bother to look at the Camel, the old fortress. I never wanted to see any of this again.

She flew west on autopilot, a few hundred feet above the desert floor. There were mountain ranges ahead of us. She used the night-vision goggles to spot them and climbed when the terrain forced her to. I dozed beside her in the copilot's seat.

Hours later she shook me awake. Out the window ahead I could see the lights of Tangier.

She had the plane on autopilot, flying toward the city. We went aft, put on coveralls, helped each other don backpacks and parachutes, then she waddled forward to check how the plane was flying.

The idea was to fly over the city from east to west, jump over the western edge of the city, and let the plane fly on, out to sea. When the fuel in the plane was exhausted it would go into the ocean, probably break up and sink.

Meanwhile we would be on our way via commercial airliner. I had my American passports in my backpack—

my real one and Robert Arnold's—and a plane ticket to South Africa. I hadn't asked Julie where she was going when we hit the ground because I didn't want to know. By that point I hoped to God I never set eyes on her again.

She lowered the tailgate, and I walked out on it. She was looking out one of the windows. She held up a hand, signaling me to get ready. I could just glimpse lights.

Now she came over to stand beside me. "Fifteen seconds," she shouted, and looked at her watch. I looked at mine, too.

I must have relaxed for just a second, because the next thing I knew she pushed me and I was going out, reaching for her. She was inches beyond my grasp.

Then I was out of the plane and falling through the darkness.

Needless to say, I never saw Julie Giraud again. I landed on a rocky slope, a sheep pasture I think, on the edge of town, and gathered up the parachute. She was nowhere in sight.

I took off my helmet, listened for airplane noise . . . nothing.

Just a distant jet, maybe an airliner leaving the commercial airport.

I buried the chute and helmet and coveralls in a hole I dug with a folding shovel. I tossed the shovel into the hole and filled it with my hands, tromped it down with my new civilian shoes, then set off downhill with a flashlight. Didn't see a soul.

The next morning I walked into town and got a room at a decent hotel. I had a hot bath and went to bed and slept the clock around, almost twenty-four hours. When I awoke I went to the airport and caught a flight to Capetown.

Capetown is a pretty city in a spectacular setting, on the ocean with Table Mountain behind it. I had plenty of cash and I established an account with a local bank, then had money wired in from Switzerland. There was three million in the Swiss account before my first transfer, so Julie Giraud made good on her promise. As I instinctively knew she would.

I lived in a hotel the first week, then found a little place that a widow rented to me.

I watched the paper pretty close, expecting to see a story about the massacre in the Libyan desert. The Libyans were bound to find the wreckage of those jets sooner or later, and the bodies, and the news would leak out.

But it didn't.

The newspapers never mentioned it.

Finally I got to walking down to the city library and reading the papers from Europe and the United States.

Nothing. *Nada.*

Like it never happened.

A month went by, a peaceful, quiet month. No one paid any attention to me, I had a mountain of money in the local bank and in Switzerland, and neither radio, television, nor newspapers ever mentioned all those dead people in the desert.

Finally I called my retired Marine pal Bill Wiley in Van Nuys, the police dispatcher. "Hey, Bill, this is Charlie Dean."

"Hey, Charlie. When you coming home, guy?"

"I don't know. How's Candy doing with the stations?"

"They're making more money than they ever did with you running them. He's got rid of the facial iron and works twelve hours a day."

"No shit!"

"So where are you?"

"Let's skip that for a bit. I want you to do me a favor. Tomorrow at work how about running me on the crime computer, see if I'm wanted for anything."

He whistled. "What the hell you been up to, Charlie?"

"Will you do that? I'll call you tomorrow night."

"Give me your birth date and social security number."

I gave it to him, then said good-bye.

I was on pins and needles for the next twenty-four hours. When I called again, Bill said, "You ain't in the big computer, Charlie. What the hell you been up to?"

"I'll tell you all about it sometime."

"So when you coming home?"

"One of these days. I'm still vacationing as hard as I can."

"Kiss her once for me," Bill Wiley said.

. . .

At the Capetown library I got into old copies of the *International Herald Tribune*, published in Paris. I finally found what I was looking for on microfiche: a complete list of the passengers who died twelve years ago on the Air France flight that blew up over Niger. Colonel Giraud and his wife were not on the list.

Well, the light finally began to dawn.

I got one of the librarians to help me get on the Internet. What I was interested in were lists of U.S. Air Force Academy graduates, say from five to ten years ago.

I read the names until I thought my eyeballs were going to fall out. No Julie Giraud.

I'd been had. Julie was either a CIA or French agent. French, I suspected, and the Americans agreed to let her steal a plane.

As I sat and thought about it, I realized that I didn't ever meet old Colonel Giraud's kids. Not to the best of my recollection. Maybe he had a couple of daughters, maybe he didn't, but damned if I could remember.

What had she said? That the colonel said I was the best Marine in the corps?

Stupid ol' Charlie Dean. I ate that shit with a spoon. The best Marine in the corps! So I helped her "steal" a plane and kill a bunch of convicted terrorists that Libya would never extradite.

If we were caught I would have sworn under torture, until my very last breath, that no government was involved, that the people planning this escapade were a U.S. Air Force deserter and a former Marine she hired.

I loafed around Capetown for a few more days, paid my bills, thanked the widow lady, gave her a cock-and-bull story about my sick kids in America, and took a plane to New York. At JFK I got on another plane to Los Angeles.

When the taxi dropped me at my apartment, I stopped by the super's office and paid the rent. The battery in my car had enough juice to start the motor on the very first crank.

I almost didn't recognize Candy. He had even gotten a haircut and wore clean jeans. "Hey, Mr. Dean," Candy said after we had been chatting awhile. "Thanks for giving me another chance. You've taught me a lot."

"We all make mistakes," I told him. If only he knew how true that was.

ABOUT THE AUTHOR

Stephen Coonts is the author of sixteen *New York Times* bestsellers that have been translated and published around the world. A former naval aviator and Vietnam combat veteran, Coonts is a graduate of West Virginia University and the University of Colorado School of Law. He makes his home in Colorado.

Visit his website at www.coonts.com.